The Life of Your Time

Steven J. Byers

Muddy Road Communications
Rich Hill, Missouri

© 2001 by Steven J. Byers

All rights reserved. No part of this publication may be reproduced, stored in a retrieval system, or transmitted in any way by any means—electronic, mechanical, photocopy, recording, or otherwise—without the prior permission of the copyright holder, except brief passages quoted by reviewers and as otherwise provided by US copyright law.

Printed in the United States of America

ISBN 0-9718699-0-1
Library of Congress Catalog Card Number: 00-110718

Published by Muddy Road Communications.

Front cover art by David Paul Logan. All rights reserved by Muddy Road Communications.

Contents

Prologue: **The Inner View**..5

Chapter 1: A Clock That Could Stop a Face............11

Chapter 2: Demeaning of Life...................................23

Chapter 3: Astrayed Line..33

Chapter 4: Home on Derange....................................41

Chapter 5: Paradigms Lost...51

Chapter 6: Computer Bugs and
  Hard Drive Crashes......................................65

Chapter 7: Screen Savor...77

Chapter 8: New Whirled Order.................................93

Chapter 9: Call of the Mild.....................................109

Chapter 10: Behind the Seen...................................125

Epilogue: After Taste..149

Prologue

The Inner View

Author: So, you're interested in the position.
Narrator: Unreservedly, sir.
Author: Great. Uh, please just relax. I know interviews can be stressful.
Narrator: In what way?
Author: Well, an interview is such an artificial situation. You know, all focused on promoting yourself. It can be very stiff and uncomfortable, don't you agree?
Narrator: Is this a trick question?
Author: Excuse me?
Narrator: What I mean to say is that if I agree with your statement, it might tend to indicate that I lack poise under pressure. But if I disagree with the proposition, that could be construed as evidence that I enjoy promoting myself and that I am altogether lacking in the virtue of humility.
Author: Sorry, I wasn't trying to trip you up. I just want you to feel at ease.
Narrator: Well, then. I feel quite at ease. Thank you.
Author: Okay, let's talk about your qualifications. Have you had much experience as a narrator?
Narrator: Oh, yes. Extensive experience. Why, I have worked with some of the best authors in the business.

Author: For instance?
Narrator: *Prohibited Relationship* by Maude Linflouph.
Author: Can't say I'm familiar with that one.
Narrator: The original title was *Forbidden Love,* but that had already been used. How about *Beached Whale Beach Party* by Irving Purvis? It was a big hit with the early environmentalists.
Author: Never heard of it.
Narrator: Surely you must have read *The Bearded Lady and the Barber?* Stream-of-consciousness piece back in the '60s. Very popular with the beatniks in the coffee shop scene . . .
Author: These all sound like older books. What have you done recently?
Narrator: I did a radio spot last year to promote the hogcalling contest at the Iowa State Fair.
Author: That's it?
Narrator: Things have been a bit slow lately, I will admit. But I am confident that something will turn up soon.
Author: I checked your references.
Narrator: Splendid! I'm sure they were impeccable.
Author: Three out of the four didn't return my phone calls.
Narrator: And the fourth?
Author: She was generally favorable, though she did say you tended to be a bit verbose—
Narrator: I'm sure she meant *articulate.*
Author: . . . And opinionated.
Narrator: I prefer to think of myself as being a person of strong convictions.
Author: Perhaps that's why work has been scarce. They seem to want a lighter touch these days. Anyway, I'm not too concerned about recent expe-

The Inner View

rience as long as your skills aren't rusty. How are you on dialects—especially midwestern ones?
Narrator: I'm certified in thirty-seven.
Author: Do you do hick?
Narrator: Shore do. I'm fixin' to worsh my clothes 'cause they're plumb dirty.
Author: Hillbilly?
Narrator: Pass me that there jug o' moonshine.
Author: Not bad. But what about voices? Can you do a suburban housewife?
Narrator: Could you direct me to the mall?
Author: Disaffected Gen Xer?
Narrator: Whatever!
Author: Russian revolutionist?
Narrator: There are no Russian revolutionists in this story.
Author: Just checking. So I take it you have read the manuscript.
Narrator: Yes, sir.
Author: And what did you think?
Narrator: Quality work!
Author: Well thank you . . .
Narrator: For a first novel.
Author: Meaning?
Narrator: Oh—oh nothing. I meant that your lack of experience hardly shows in most places.
Author: Thanks a lot.
Narrator: This is going badly, isn't it.
Author: Uh, no. Actually, the job is yours if you want it.
Narrator: Magnificent! But, out of all the great narrators you could have chosen, why did you pick me?
Author: You're the only one who applied. After all, I'm no C. S. Lewis.

The Life of Your Time

Narrator: And I am no Orson Welles. But I shall endeavor to the utmost to fulfill the trust you have placed in me. When do we begin?

Author: Now would be a good time. The reader has already joined us.

Narrator: Oh, I see. Stupendous! I am ready to begin if you are. Once upon a time . . .

Author: This isn't a fairy tale.

Narrator: Of course. My exuberance temporarily overwhelmed me.

Author: And one other thing, if you don't mind. Please be conservative with the superlatives. You've already used "splendid," "magnificent," "stupendous" and "exuberance," and we haven't even begun the story. I can't afford an unabridged thesaurus and I don't want to run out of descriptive words.

Narrator: I quite understand, sir, and shall strive to contain myself.

Author: Good.

Narrator: If I may interject one more thing before we begin, though. "Superlative" refers to adjectives and adverbs. "Exuberance" is a noun, so it would be grammatically incorrect . . .

Author: Would you mind getting on with it?

Narrator: This is a story about the meaning of life—whether there is one and, if so, what it might be. There are no superheroes, epic battles, dragon slayings, car chases, gratuitous violence or salacious scenes. In fact, the characters are, for the most part, ordinary everyday people. Although you, dear reader, do not yet know them, they may strike you as being familiar—the kind you could very well meet tomorrow at school or work. Though their lives may seem superficially mundane, each faces struggles of various kinds. While

The Inner View

these personal quests may not seem on the surface to be as virtuous as slaying dragons or conquering armies, they are, nevertheless, of utmost significance to those involved. The fact that none of them are endowed with any superpowers whatsoever only heightens the sense of suspense. After all, superheroes always win in the end. For mere mortals, however, the outcome is less predictable.

Chapter 1

A Clock That Could Stop a Face

"What time is it?" the man asked impatiently. "My watch has stopped."

The woman glanced around and replied, "The clock over there says 1:14."

The man looked in the direction she had indicated and said, "That's not a clock. That's a picture of a clock." He turned to a boy standing nearby and said, "Hey, kid. Do you have the time?"

The boy looked at his watch. "It's 1:14, sir."

The man started to protest, but the boy held up the watch for him to see and, yes, the cartoon hands of his watch were very definitely in the 1:14 position. "Right. Well . . . uh . . . thanks."

"You're very welcome, sir," the boy said as the couple wandered off around the divider. The lad looked again at the still life painting of the clock and said to himself, "That's strange."

The boy's name was Percival Weckbaugh. To the untrained eye, he would have appeared to be an unremarkable sixth-grader—slight build, fine mousy hair, and glasses that were a bit on the thick side for his age. But those who by diligent practice have trained themselves to penetrate beyond superficial appearances would see much more in Percival. And since you, the reader, are obviously one of those people, nothing more need be said along those lines at this point. However, just in case some unauthorized person (that is, an insensitive, unfeeling sort) is reading this story, even you should be able to pick up on Percival's most distinguishing characteristic—that he was extraordinarily polite, which is fairly uncommon today in the general population and practically unheard of among sixth graders.

It was a Thursday in Central City. The reason Percival happened to be at this particular point in space and time and not another was that he was covering the school art fair in the hope that he could get the write-up published in the *Central Citizen*. Normally, only high school students wrote articles for the *Citizen*, with occasional contributions from gifted junior high school kids. So getting his first article published as a sixth-grader was a real coup—not that Percival was an exceptional writer or consumed with ambition in this respect. The article actually started out as a class essay on the topic of line etiquette. Although he was biased toward the existing rules, he tried to present the issues fairly—how the daily leaders were determined, whether it was appropriate to whisper while standing in the hall, why you should avoid touching the person next to you and the dangers of dawdling or running in line formation.

The most controversial point, as you might suspect, was cutting in line—particularly the old front-cut/back-cut trick. He was especially tough on that one because of the menace to society it posed. Oh, it looked innocent enough. In fact, it even had an outward appearance of politeness by seemingly putting someone else's needs ahead of your own. The deception was that it was committed in the expectation that

A Clock That Could Stop A Face

the favor would be immediately returned. Percival argued convincingly that this was nothing more than a sham because the net effect on the accomplice was nil and the perpetrator, in actuality, was just crowding in front of the person behind the accomplice without permission, thereby harming all the other people in line from that point back. When practiced by groups, the line culture degenerated to anarchy. Percival concluded that section decisively: "Cutting is cutting, no matter how you slice it." Although he did not intend the pun when he wrote it, he was rather pleased with it when he noticed it later. Perhaps he should have pointed out that it was accidental when people commented on his cleverness, but most people would not have faulted him because he did not.

His teacher Mrs. Thomas liked the essay very much—so much so that she shared it with Miss Pickett, the journalism advisor. Miss Pickett taught English, grammar, composition, literature and related subjects and had considerable expertise in this area, though her experience did not go all the way back to the invention of these things as many of her students supposed.

Being from a generation where manners were more highly regarded than they are today, Miss Pickett was especially taken with the essay. Even though the writing was more than a bit sixth-graderish, she recognized its potential and decided to work with Percival on re-writing the piece for inclusion on the editorial page of the *Central Citizen*. She helped him undangle a few participles and tighten up his argument here and there. She had, let us say, a fondness for the intricacies of grammar. The less grateful of her students felt it was more on the order of obsession and called her "Miss Picky," though never to her face. Percival did not mind, though. On the contrary, he was flattered that she was interested in his work and warmed by the fact that she shared his appreciation of good manners. The result was that while still essentially his own work, the finished piece had a moderately mature ring to it. In fact, with her fine tuning, it was as good or better than some of the work her high school students were doing. The quality of that writing, she believed, was declining in inverse proportion to the amount of television each successive generation of kids was watching. And she was probably right.

The reaction among Percival's peers was mixed. The more emotionally secure were proud that one of their classmates had made it to the big leagues, though they would have been far more impressed if it had been the varsity basketball team. The less charitable accused him of trying to curry favor with the teachers by writing what they wanted to hear. Their criticism was tempered by the fact that Percival had argued for a special exemption to the strict no-cutting policy for anyone with a broken leg. This, of course, scored major points with the more politically correct students and even the teachers had to acknowledge the wisdom of this. The principal declared that this had always been the policy at the school and blamed the omission of the broken leg clause from the written conduct policy on a clerical error.

The habitual line cutters viewed this as a major concession—not that the policy was enforced rigorously anyway. Only flagrant violators were ever reprimanded and the usual punishment was being sent to the back of the line—the very place they had come from originally. Basically, they had nothing to lose and everything to gain. The game, therefore, was obviously about something more than just getting a better place in line since they were doing that any-

A Clock That Could Stop A Face

way. The plain and simple fact was they just did not like rules in general—unless, of course, they could be worked to their own advantage. Thus, they began to exploit the broken leg loophole to include a variety of other situations and, within a few days, were even trying to make the case that being extremely hungry or thirsty or anxious to go to recess were seriously handicapping conditions.

Percival had never fancied himself a journalist before nor did he necessarily perceive this one editorial as a sign for a life's calling. But he had to admit that there was something self-affirming and perhaps even exhilarating about seeing one's name in print, especially when you are not the most popular kid in school.

Now to say that Percival was not the most popular kid should not be interpreted that he was disliked. After all, it is hard to actively dislike someone who is extraordinarily polite—unless, of course, they are polite in an annoying way. That sort of politeness, though, is not really politeness at all. For some it is a neurotic condition of the type you see occasionally in a mother who drives her family away with her own version of kindness by "working my fingers to the bone" (and constantly reminding them of it) and then savors feeling sorry for herself because no one appears adequately grateful and her kids do not phone home very often. At another extreme is the sort of politeness that is sometimes observed in salesmen, politicians, fund raisers and religious people right before they do something that is not in keeping with that same spirit of politeness. Fortunately, this type of politeness is transparent even to those who are only moderately discerning and automatically alerts the hearer's defense mechanisms.

The Life of Your Time

None of these applied to Percival. He was polite in the genuine, inoffensive way and therein lay the cause of his lack of popularity. It was not that he was disliked as much as he was ignored. It is an often-overlooked fact that most popular people have a knack for putting themselves forward (almost by definition)—so much so that a person who is both extremely popular and extremely humble is extremely rare. The ironic thing about putting oneself forward is that it must be practiced skillfully in order to avoid detection or it is likely to have the opposite effect and lead to a decrease in popularity. Some master the art and climb to great heights of notoriety. Far more would like to, but are clumsier at it or lack certain prerequisites such as good looks, athletic ability, brains or charm. These folks paint a rather pathetic picture but, when you think about it, probably no more so than those who put themselves forward successfully.

Being extraordinarily polite, Percival was not one to put himself forward—successfully or unsuccessfully. Therefore, he tended to fade into the background of anonymity—to stand perennially in the rear of the line of life. So this particular moment in his existence was very satisfying to him because he had been temporarily exalted above his peers, not by pushing himself forward, but because he had taken a stand for what he thought was right. There seemed to be justice in that—a sense that something had gone right in the universe. He rather enjoyed the feeling and most people would not fault him for that.

So when he overheard Miss Pickett say that none of the regular *Citizen* staff wanted to cover the school art fair, he volunteered. While it had seemed like a good idea at the time, he now felt like he was in over his head. At least he had known what he was talking about when he wrote about line etiquette, but he did

A Clock That Could Stop A Face

not know the first thing about art. Oh, he liked the pictures and the sculptures, but he was at a loss to explain why some received blue ribbons and others only participant ribbons. Some looked very much like the objects they represented, while others were unrecognizable shapes and colors. A more pressing problem presented itself when he tried to write about them. He could describe them in general way, but when he read what he had written, he realized that he was coming nowhere close to what they were really all about. He thought, "It's like trying to . . .", but he could not finish the thought because he did not really know what it *was* like. He only knew that it was frustrating and he decided that being a writer was not easy.

He had been standing in the middle of the school multipurpose room feeling befuddled. The tables and dividers had been arranged at angles rather than rows which gave the normally familiar room a rather maze-like quality. The disorienting sensation was heightened by the blending of many voices—students and visitors—into one big unintelligible buzzing. He had been looking for the exit and wondering what laboratory mice felt like. For a moment, he thought he even caught a whiff of rancid cheese, but it turned out to be Billy Smith, who was no candidate to win the good hygiene award. He had been standing there debating on whether to follow Billy's trail out when the clock incident occurred.

This strange occurrence, though, had temporarily caused him to forget all about his writing frustrations as well as how silly he felt about being lost in a room he had been in hundreds of times. It had set his mind to thinking. And these thoughts were not the ordinary, everyday kind. No, these were special thoughts that only very special people think. He stood in front of the clock picture for a long time . . .

Narrator: Excuse me, aren't you going to tell the reader what Percival was thinking?
Author: I can't.
Narrator: Why not?
Author: Because they were thoughts that don't translate very well into words. It would be like Percival trying to write about the art at the show. Sometimes language is inadequate to communicate certain thoughts just like the nose is inadequate to perceive music. Besides, as a sensitive and discerning person, the reader is probably already beginning to think some of those very same thoughts.
Narrator (whispering): What if the reader is not sensitive and discerning?
Author: I can't explain it, but I feel as though we can trust this reader.
Narrator: Hmmmm.
Author: Could we get on with the story now?
Narrator: Oh, right. Where were we?

Percival stood in front of the clock picture for a long time wondering about what had happened. He looked at his watch which now said 1:20 and back at the clock which still said 1:14. "Very strange," he said.

Then he realized he needed to get back to class, though he was still not quite sure what direction that would be. He finally had the presence of mind to look up instead of around. Once he saw the lights on the ceiling, he got his bearings and found his way out of the maze.

* * * * *

A Clock That Could Stop A Face

Percival lived in a carefully maintained Victorian house on the south edge of Central City. His parents lived there too, which was convenient because Percival, George and Ann were all quite fond of each other. It was a nice house—nothing extravagant by anyone's standards, but spacious for a family of three. So, there was no need to worry about getting in each other's way. And there was an orderliness to it that seemed to suit its occupants well.

When Percival sat down to write the art fair article that evening in his orderly house, he quickly realized he was not getting anywhere. He went downstairs into the living room where his father was reading the evening newspaper.

"Dad?"

"Yes, son," said his father as he peered out over the top of the newspaper, his bifocals slung low on his nose.

"I'm having trouble with my story on the art fair."

Mr. Weckbaugh folded the paper and laid it on the table next to his chair. "What sort of trouble?"

"When I try to write about the pictures, it doesn't sound like what the pictures really were. It's like trying to . . ." His voice trailed off because he still did not know what it was like.

His father waited patiently for Percival to finish the sentence for he was a polite person, too. But after a long pause, he realized that Percival was not going to finish it. He guessed that was the point of the conversation, so he offered, "Like trying to smell music?"

"Smell music?"

"Music is experienced by the ears, not the nose. And pictures are experienced by the eyes, not through words. Sometimes, language just isn't adequate to communicate certain kinds of thoughts."

The Life of Your Time

Percival nodded slowly as he recognized the wisdom of that. "You're really smart, Dad. How do you know all these things?"

Now it was George Weckbaugh's turn to be puzzled. At fifty-two, he was older than all the fathers of Percival's classmates, and with his sparse hair now substantially gray, he was often mistaken for his grandfather. His occupation was that of computer systems analyst and he momentarily got that far-away look that sometimes crossed his face when he was working on an especially knotty problem. "I don't know, son. It just popped into my head."

"So what should I do?"

"You know I'm not in the habit of telling people what to do," said his father. "But when I'm trying to solve a problem, I begin by trying to sort out the known facts and see how far it takes me. Start with what you know for certain and usually you can figure out the rest."

That seemed like reasonable advice as Percival thought about how to approach the article. Mr. Weckbaugh, thinking the conversation had ended, started to reach for his newspaper. But there was more on Percival's mind.

"Something else happened today and I wanted to ask you about it," he said. "There was a man who asked his wife what time it was. She told him it was 1:14 because she looked at a picture of a clock. Then he asked me what time it was and when I looked at my watch, it really was 1:14."

"And . . .?"

"That's it."

"I'm afraid I don't understand what the question is."

"Well, what does it mean?"

A Clock That Could Stop A Face

"That it was 1:14?" Mr. Weckbaugh could see by the look on Percival's face that he was not satisfied by that answer. "Sorry. Does it mean something to you?"

"I don't know yet."

Just then, Percival's mother called from the kitchen, "Supper's ready."

"We'd better go. We don't want to keep your mother waiting," said Mr. Weckbaugh. Then he added, "I'll give it some thought."

"Thanks Dad."

* * * * *

Every 487 years or so, the elliptical orbit of a seemingly insignificant bit of iron carried it to within a few hundred thousand miles from earth—a near miss in the cosmic sense. Three revolutions ago, however, it passed close enough to Jupiter that the planet's gravitational field caused an infinitesimally small wobble in its trajectory. But infinitesimally small wobbles have a way of becoming magnified over vast expanses of space and time. So, after an untold number of circuits around the solar system, the current one was destined to be its last as it careened its way toward earth.

Chapter 2

Demeaning of Life

The next day was Friday and Percival let Mrs. Thomas read his article before he turned it into Miss Pickett. He had decided to take his father's advice and stick to the facts. He gave an overview of the art fair—when and where it was held, how many students participated and who the winners were in each category—and then tacked on a quote from the art teacher who coordinated the event about how everyone who participated was a winner. Percival wondered if the kids who received only a certificate of participation would agree with that sentiment, but he did not speculate on it in print. Anyway, once he had decided upon the practical approach, the assignment had not proved to be overly difficult.

While Mrs. Thomas was reading, Percival inadvertantly yawned. He tried to stifle it, but that, of course, is very nearly impossible, so all he could do was excuse himself. The yawn reminded him of his restless night. A most disquieting dream had interrupted his slumber and he had not slept well after that. He could not remember what the dream was about and that disturbed him.

"That's good, Percival," said Mrs. Thomas, but she did not offer any suggestions. A person more cynical than Percival might have wondered if it was because it really was good or if she was not giving it her full attention—the latter possibility evidenced by the fact that she kept looking around the classroom every few seconds to see who was whispering. It is an unfortunate reality in schools that students generally get an average of a mere 1/25 of the teacher's attention. The only ones who get more are the troublemakers and the ones who are skilled at putting themselves forward. This attention, of course, comes at the expense of the quiet students' shares. Truly superior teachers, if you will notice, resolve this dilemma by giving each student their full attention for 1/25 of their time and generally good results are seen when it is the time, rather than the attention, which is divided.

"There was something else I wanted to ask you about," said Percival. "There was a man who asked his wife what time it was. She told him it was 1:14 because she looked at a picture of a clock. Then he asked me what time it was and when I looked at my watch, it really was 1:14." He paused, waiting for her to respond.

Mrs. Thomas was having prescient flashes of a spitwad about to be shot. She looked up to see Freddie Lake frozen like a back-to-school-sale mannequin in perfect deskwork posture. She was not fooled, of course, and stared menacingly at him. He returned a "Who me?" shrug. This was given sincerely in the knowledge that he would not dare to do such a dastardly deed. However, he felt no compunction that only moments before he had, in fact, been trying to entice smelly Billy Smith into doing his dirty work for him by launching his doomsday missile into the strawberry-blonde hair of the girl who sat in front of him. Mrs. Thomas was good, they grudgingly acknowledged to themselves. Very good. So the mission was temporarily aborted and Mrs. Thomas

Demeaning of Life

turned again to Percival. "Excuse me? Oh, yes. That's an interesting coincidence."

"What's a coincidence?" asked Percival.

"It's when two things happen at the same time or the same place that seem to be connected but aren't," Mrs. Thomas answered.

"But what does it mean?" asked Percival.

"What does what mean?"

"The coincidence."

"It doesn't mean anything," she said. "That's why it's called a coincidence. If it meant something, it wouldn't be a coincidence."

"What would it be?"

"Don't you need to be studying your spelling words?" suggested Mrs. Thomas. "We're getting ready to have the final test."

"I got them all right on Wednesday," Percival replied.

"Are you feeling well?"

"Yes, ma'am. I'm feeling fine." Percival thought for a moment. "Well, maybe I am a little tired. I didn't sleep well last night. But thank you for asking."

"Aha!" said Mrs. Thomas. "You're just over-tired. That's all. Go lay your head on your desk for a little while. I need to grade papers."

Random Number: Hi! I'm a random number, but you can call me 1314. I thought I would interject myself here in a completely meaningless place. That's what we random numbers do. We're always popping up unpredictably, what with Blind Chance running the show and all. Which raises some interesting questions: Was Blind Chance born blind or did he lose his sight later? Is he truly blind or just short-sighted? Does he get any royalties from the red cards in Monopoly . . . ?

The Life of Your Time

Narrator: How rude! Sir, do you realize you have interrupted my telling of this story?
Random Number: What difference does it make?
Narrator: Well, it is going to make it more difficult for the reader to connect what went on before with what goes on after.
Random Number: Great! Then I've succeeded. After all, that's what randomness is supposed to do—break up people's silly notions that anything in life is connected in a meaningful way to anything else. It's great work, when you can get it. But it's rather sporadic—occupational hazard, I guess. Oh, it used to be better back when I was getting lots of scientific work. That is, until I got kicked out of the Scientific Random Numbers Union over that one silly little incident. Now I'm just a lonely free floater.
Narrator: Just out of curiosity, what was the one silly little incident?
Random Number: Oops! I've said too much. If Blind Chance finds out I've been talking to you, he'll be furious. I'll get demoted to the Unlucky Numbers division for sure. Ever heard of 13? He's been there for a long time now. And what about 666? I don't want to get stuck with those losers. I'm out of here!
Narrator: Dear reader, please excuse the unexpected interruption to the story. We will pick up where we left off.

After lunch, there was a knock at the door of the classroom. Mr. Wimbley timidly peeked inside the door and exchanged a look with Mrs. Thomas. Then she said, "Percival, I'd like for you to come with me for a few minutes. I have . . . uh, an errand for you to run."

Demeaning of Life

Outside in the hallway, Mrs. Thomas said, "Percival, you need to go with Mr. Wimbley for a little while."

Percival was perplexed. "Did I do something wrong?"

"Oh, no," she said. "It's just that he is more qualified to handle these . . . situations than I am."

Percival quickly found himself sitting on a piece of vinyl and stainless steel furniture of the sort that is never seen outside of institutions. It resembled a chair to the extent that one might mistakenly call it that—until you sat on it. It was breathtakingly cold in the winter but made you sweat any other time of the year. Percival was very uncomfortable in the thing because if he leaned back, his feet stuck straight out and if he sat forward, his feet still didn't touch the ground so that he just had to balance himself on the edge. And every time he moved slightly, the vinyl made embarrassing noises.

Not only was he uncomfortable in the so-called chair, he was even more uncomfortable with the idea of being there. You see, Mr. Wimbley was the school counselor. Percival had seen him before because he was the one who administered the standardized achievement tests. But Percival had never been in his office before and that made him nervous. Only kids with problems got sent there.

"Just relax, P.J.," said Mr. Wimbley in a nasally tone. Since relaxing was impossible, Percival just nodded and smiled weakly. It struck Percival as odd that this man who was all but a stranger would even know that some of the kids called him P.J. His middle name was James, so some of the kids used the nickname "P.J."—a practice he neither encouraged nor discouraged, though it sounded strange now coming out of the mouth of a grown-up. A person of lesser character might have preferred a nickname over the name Percival, but since it had been his name all his life, he was rather accustomed to it. Besides, his mother had told him that Percival was one of the brave Knights of the Round Table in the Arthurian legend and he liked the sound of "Sir Percival." Though he never told anyone, he sometimes fantasized that he *was* this brave knight slaying dragons, rescuing distressed damsels and valiantly upholding the chivalric code.

The name "Percival," however, was a bit of a mouthful for some of the kids, so they sometimes called him P.J. He would not have minded at all except that when he was in the third grade, Freddie Lake and some of the other boys in his class took to teasing him with "Pajama Boy" and "P.J. wears his mama's pajamas" which, of course, was not true. That had been the closest he had ever come to wanting to punch someone, but he knew that would be wrong— not to mention impolite. The only alternative he could think of was to ignore them, which he did. Actually, this proved to be a very wise strategy. Since the boys could not get any kind of reaction out of him, it did not turn out to be a very good sport and they soon lost interest. Naturally, he was very relieved when they did. Ever since, he had been carefully neutral about the use of P.J. And he was very thankful his middle name was not Patrick.

"Now P.J., I'd like to uh . . . chat with you for a few minutes," said Mr. Wimbley. He was a smallish man with a thin mustache that accented his thin lips. "So, is everything okay at home?"

"Yes, sir."

"Are your mother and father doing well?"

"Quite well, thank you."

"They're not divorced are they?"

"No, sir."

Demeaning of Life

"Are you currently seeing a therapist?"

It took a moment for the question to register. Then Percival said, "No, sir."

"Taking any medications?"

"No."

"Ever had a serious head injury?"

"No."

"Seizures?"

"No."

"Hmmmm."

Percival did not think he liked the sound of that. He mustered his courage and interjected his own question into the pause. "Why are you asking me all these questions?"

"Oh, these are just routine questions we ask in cases like these," said Mr. Wimbley. "We just want to identify the source of the problem."

"Problem?"

"Mrs. Thomas said you were behaving strangely in class today."

All Percival could think of was when he told her about the clock incident. "Because I asked her a question?"

"It was more the nature of the question," said Mr. Wimbley.

"All I did was tell her about something that happened and asked her if she thought it meant anything. Is that bad?"

"Well," he said in a tone that some might have construed as bordering on sarcasm, "you might as well ask, 'What is the meaning of life?'"

"Exactly!"

"I was speaking rhetorically," said Mr. Wimbley, though the subtle tonal shadings between academic rhetoric and sarcasm might have been difficult for a mere layperson to distinguish.

"Right," said Percival, having no idea what "rhetorically" meant. "I guess I was thinking that if this one thing meant something, then other things might mean something and maybe everything means something."

"P.J., people don't usually go around asking questions like that," said Mr. Wimbley.

"Why not?" asked Percival.

"It's not . . . normal."

"I see," said Percival. "But is that because life does mean something and everyone knows it so they don't need to ask? Or is it because life doesn't mean anything so there is no point talking about it?"

Mr. Wimbley scribbled on his notepad and squirmed in his chair, his bowtie flitting like a butterfly. Trying to regain the upper hand in the conversation, he said, "You're missing the point, P.J. The real issue here is your recent behavior which I believe is a cry for attention because you don't feel good about yourself."

"I don't?"

"I mean, I see it all the time," said Mr. Wimbley. "Oh, it manifests itself in different ways, but it always boils down to self-esteem. That's it. Building self-esteem is a big part of what the educational system is designed to do—help you discover who you are and to feel good about it."

"What if you are a bad person?" asked Percival.

"There are no bad people," Mr. Wimbley said. "Deep down, everyone has a heart of gold. They just need to find it and let it shine."

"Even a murderer?"

"That's a perfect example of what happens when someone feels bad about himself—he acts out in violence," Mr. Wimbley explained. "But, if somewhere along the way, someone would have helped him over-

Demeaning of Life

come those negative feelings, he could have been a productive member of society instead of ending up in prison." One might call it a blessing and another a stroke of luck that Percival could not read the note Mr. Wimbley had written to himself being, as it were, upside down at an upward angle from a distance of about six feet. Therefore, he was spared the indignity of reading, "PA (passive aggressive) Subject's polite facade masks inner hostility toward authority. Obvious low SE (self-esteem). Order psych. eval. (psychiatric evaluation)."

Percival pondered all that Mr. Wimbley had said. He thought about his classmates, many of whom did seem to feel very good about themselves. It also occurred to him that the ones who liked themselves most were among the ones he liked the least. In fact, these were often the very same ones who were always crowding in line and putting themselves forward in various ways. Could he have been wrong about them? "I see," he said.

Now Percival meant this as, "I hear what you're saying," not "I agree with what you're saying," and there is obviously a huge difference between the two. Mr. Wimbley, however, because he was anxious to turn the corner on the discussion, took it as the latter. "Good. That's what you need, P.J., a healthy dose of self-esteem and your problems will be solved."

"Thank you for taking time to explain this to me," Percival said. Then he added, "I'm starting to feel better already."

Now a person of strict moral standards might be quick to condemn Percival for that last statement because it implied that he agreed with Mr. Wimbley's whole argument, which was not true since he was actually undecided. A pragmatist, however, would defend him on the grounds that the desperate nature of the situation justified it. This view would have been strengthened by the fact that as soon as Percival said it, Mr. Wimbley crossed out "Order psych. eval." and wrote, "Subject making progress. Continue to monitor," thus sparing him from countless hours in therapy that might have really messed him up.

Actually, neither of these views applied in Percival's case. He simply had sensed the "chat" was drawing to a close, and in the spirit of the conversation was merely expressing his relief that the ordeal was over.

Chapter 3

Astrayed Line

The afternoon was passing and it was not long before it was time for the last recess. The children lined up in the hallway as they prepared to go outside. As usual, certain kids crowded to the front as soon as the teacher's back was turned. Also, as usual, Percival found himself at the end of the line.

But then something very unusual happened. In fact, it had never happened before. A look came over Percival's face—a very determined look. There was a first step which was followed by a second. Then he was marching toward the exit, making no attempt whatsoever to be sly or conceal his movements. By the time he reached the door, the eyes of all the students were on him. They were so shocked that no one even protested when he . . . well, there is no good way to say it except to just come right out with it: Percival cut to the very front of the line!

If the thoughts that Percival began thinking at 1:14 Thursday had a dark counterpart, it would be the thoughts he was thinking now—thoughts that were so raw and primitive that they scarcely qualified as thoughts. So hot and wild were these feelings that they began to melt something in his heart—something that might be described as innocence. If this phenomenon could have been observed in space and time, it would have appeared to ooze out of his heart and drip onto the pea-green tiled floor at Central City Elementary School.

Strangely enough, Mrs. Thomas did not even notice. Her misbehavior detector was tuned to the sneaky frequency. That is to say she could hear a barely audible whisper thirty feet away or sense the passing of a note while her back was turned. Oh, it was a gift, to be sure, one which even some of the other teachers coveted. But it came at the expense of filtering out less subtle distractions—the logic probably being that people who do bad things do not want to be caught so anyone who is making no effort to not get caught must not be doing anything wrong. To say that a student could have constructed a bomb and detonated it in the classroom without her noticing, as long as it was in plain view with each step explained out loud, would be an exaggeration. But probably not by much.

The act did not go completely unnoticed by adults, however. Mrs. Thomas might have called it a coincidence and others might have called it something else, but who should walk out of the teachers' lounge at that exact moment? Miss Pickett!

Now it was not so much that he knew he was going to get in trouble. And it was not the fact that his brief career as a journalist seemed to be going down in flames. No, the thing that struck Percival most clearly and profoundly at that moment was the look of shock and disappointment that was beginning to form on Miss Pickett's face. It was a look that penetrated right to Percival's heart. And what had previously been only a tiny hole in the fabric of time and space became a giant rip.

But before Miss Pickett could utter the words she was having difficulty formulating in her mind, the girl in line behind him said, "It's okay, Miss Pickett. It's Percival's turn to be the leader today." The gasps of the other children when they saw Miss Pickett had broken through the threshold of Mrs. Thomas' awareness and she headed toward the front of the line. The girl then said, "Isn't that right, Mrs. Thomas. Percival is the leader today."

The girl spoke with such authority that Mrs. Thomas assumed she must know what she was talking about. Actually, Mrs. Thomas had no idea if that was, in fact, the case. She just made out the line leader schedule, posted it once each quarter and did not bother to check it again unless there was a dispute. Most of the time, the kids sorted it out themselves, though if she had paid more attention she would have discovered that some got to be the leader frequently while others rarely if ever did. This was accomplished through a variety of means—bullying, blackmail, the black market (trading leader privileges for half a peanut butter sandwich and such) and sometimes, as in Percival's case, through sheer lack of attention to such matters.

Some of the braver students joined in, "Yes, Percival is the leader." This was not because they knew this or because they were sticking up for Percival as a friend. It was because they were all scared witless of Miss Pickett and would not wish her wrath on even their worst enemy. So Mrs. Thomas pronounced, "That's right, Karen. Percival is the leader today."

"Of course," said Miss Pickett, her frown melting away. "Of course. Enjoy your recess, children."

The Life of Your Time

* * * * *

The autumn afternoon air, crisp and fresh, was a welcome relief to Percival's face. He got on one of the swings, not really swinging—just mostly sitting. Other kids took turns on the adjacent swings. Before long, Karen was sitting in the swing next to his.

"How did you know today was my day to be the leader?" Percival ventured.

"I make it my business to know what goes on at this school." Karen's strawberry blonde hair hung straight down to her shoulders, and though some might have said she was a bit on the plain-looking side, her penetrating blue-gray eyes refused to be dismissed that easily. She was slightly taller than Percival, but as yet showed no hint of blossoming into womanhood as some of her peers were beginning to do. "And I know a lot about you, too. I know your birthday is January 14. I know your father works with computers. And your mother was a music major, but she doesn't work now."

"I can't believe you know all that!" said Percival, amazed.

"Like I said, I make it my business to know. But there's one thing I don't understand."

"What's that?"

"You really didn't know it was your turn to be the leader today, did you?"

Percival shook his head.

"I knew it! I could tell by the look on your face. You don't pay any attention to stuff like that. I guess that's what I don't understand. Here you are, one of the smartest kids in the class. You could go a long way in life. But if you don't mind my saying so, you lack the killer instinct."

Astrayed Line

In this respect, Karen Maddox knew what she was talking about since she was the one in their class who made the best grades. It was not necessarily that she was the smartest, but she had a combination of intelligence and drive that consistently put her on top. That is one of the reasons she found Percival so intriguing. Here was someone who could be a worthy rival, yet he seemed to have no interest at all in competing.

"My daddy says it's a jungle out there," Karen continued. "Survival of the fittest and all that. He has his own business, you know. Marketing office supplies. Grossed almost a million dollars in sales last year. That's a lot of pencils. Anyway, he says if you're going to get ahead in the world, you've got to keep that competitive edge."

"Getting ahead," Percival mused. "That's important. Isn't it?"

"Yes it is," said Karen, emphasizing each word.

"Do you think it's the *most* important thing?" asked Percival. "I mean, is that what life is all about?"

"Well, there's always family and friends and being a good citizen," she said. "But on the whole, I'd say getting ahead ranks right up there."

"I see."

Karen sensed some hesitation, so she pressed him. "Why? Do you think there is something else to it?"

"I'm not sure," said Percival. "But I've been thinking about it a lot." He started to tell her about the clock incident, but hesitated momentarily. The last time he mentioned it, he wound up in the counselor's office. On the other hand, she sounded sincerely interested and, after all, she had practically saved his life. So he told her.

"Weird," she said when he was finished.

The Life of Your Time

"That's the point," he said. "What if stuff like that doesn't just happen? What if it means something?"

"I don't know, Percival. That's pretty heavy." There was silence for a few moments. Then Karen said, "If you really didn't know it was your turn to be the leader, why did you cut to the front of the line? I thought you were against that sort of thing—like in the article you wrote."

"I just did it," said Percival, a fresh blush of shame stinging his face. "I don't really know why. Maybe I was tired of being last all the time. Only now, well—it wasn't what I thought it would be." He paused and then said, "If it really is a dog-eat-dog world, why did you stick up for me?"

Now there was a range of motivations that might have inspired a person less noble than Karen. For example, she could have done it because she knew she could eat his lunch any day of the week, and because he was no threat, she could help him without worrying about hurting herself. Even worse, she could have done it because she felt sorry for him. Worst of all, she could have done it self-righteously because "it was the right thing to do."

Thankfully, none of these motivations applied to Karen's action. She simply said, "I guess it was because I like you." With that she stood up, as recess had come to an end. "Hey, if you get this meaning of life thing figured out, you'll let me know, won't you?" He nodded to her as she turned and headed toward the building. Then he rose slowly and followed her inside.

If Percival's mind had been less preoccupied, he might have made more of her disclosure about liking him. He might have even become obsessed about it and wondered day and night what she really meant and whether she wanted him to be her boyfriend. As it was, though, he took it at face value and it registered very pleasantly in his mind. And because he did not digest the whole idea at once, it tasted sweeter in the days to come whenever his thoughts returned to it.

Chapter 4

Home on Derange

Percival did not ride the bus home that day. He was a thinker and walking is considerably superior to bus riding for thinking. His house was only about a mile from the school and his mother did not mind if he walked when the weather was nice. She knew he would not get into trouble.

Between Central Elementary School and home lay a park which Percival had found to be a splendid place for both walking and thinking. There were some tennis courts and playground equipment on the south end, but most of the rest was given over to grass and trees. It is an interesting characteristic of human nature that it has an overwhelming urge to conquer nature by hewing out cities from the wilderness. Equally interesting is the urgent need to preserve pockets of nature within civilization, whether it be house plants, yards or urban parks. Most interesting of all is man's mistaken belief that he has succeeded in either preserving or conquering nature. The former is denied by the fact that nature pockets are inevitably watered-down imitations of the original and the latter fails because the civilizing effects of man are merely an illusion. True nature, at all levels, is unconquerable by man.

Near the eastern boundary of the park was the old state insane asylum. It was a massive brick complex that in its heyday housed nearly a thousand patients at any given time. Now, though, it was mostly empty, which seemed somehow appropriate since most of its diagnostic and treatment methodologies were too. Being imprisoned with hundreds of mentally ill people in close quarters for extended periods would be enough to test even a relatively sane person. This was coupled with constant exhortations from therapists that they needed to "find themselves," despite the fact that the majority already had done that to a greater or lesser extent and the revelation had driven them to institutionalization. Add to that the vast amount of feel-good medications being dispensed that were a hindrance to clear thinking and genuine problem-solving and it was a wonder that any of them ever got better. Most did not.

When the state closed the facility, a private psychiatric hospital had leased one wing of the institution. It was a fairly small-scale operation, treating mostly self-referrals for drug and alcohol rehabilitation and nonviolent disorders. Although the company had made some modest improvements, it was still an oppressive and depressing place. Its most appealing feature was its isolation—one could seek asylum inside an institution tucked away in a small town with a fair degree of anonymity. This is for the same reason that household trash is kept in containers in out-of-the-way places—no one wants to see the waste products of civilization.

As Percival walked along, he was thinking so deeply that he did not notice the man who was mum-

Home on Derange

bling to himself, until the man exclaimed, apparently to Percival, "It's a conspiracy!"

Now most people would have walked right on by and ignored a man mumbling on a park bench so near a mental institution. Percival, however, being extraordinarily polite, could not just pass by without acknowledging someone who was speaking to him. That would be rude. On the other hand, his mother had warned him about talking to strangers and this man certainly qualified in at least two senses of the word: He was unknown to Percival and he was obviously odd. This put Percival in a dilemma. Now if the man had said, "Hello. How are you today?", he could have replied, "Fine, thank you, sir," and gone on his way—thereby being both polite and prudent. But he was at a loss to know what the courteous response was to, "It's a conspiracy!"

The man, sensing Percival's hesitation, said, "It's okay, boy. I'm a Professor. You can trust me."

That seemed reassuring, so Percival ventured, "What's a conspiracy?"

Narrator: A *conspiracy* is a secret plan to do something bad.
Author: You're interrupting the story again. I'm sure the reader already knows what a conspiracy is. And, if not, the definition may be found in any dictionary. Percival meant that he wanted to know what it was that constituted the conspiracy.
Narrator: I'm aware of that. I'm omniscient, you know.
Author: Would you like to try for limited omniscient?
Narrator: But I know what the characters are thinking, what they are going to do and how the story will end.
Author: I could always change it.

The Life of Your Time

Narrator: You can not.

Author: Says who?

Narrator: The Narrators Guild, that is who.

Author: The Narrators Guild! Narrators are storytellers. They tell the stories that authors write. Narrators are important, but the author is the one in control of the story.

Narrator: We will see about that!

Author: Yes, we will.

The reader should interpret this paragraph as representing a long interval (it cannot really be called time since it stands outside of the story and the characters are totally unaware of it) in which the Author is forced to demonstrate to the Narrator his mastery over the plot. At first, the Narrator ignores the obvious. However, as the interval drags on, the Narrator begins to squirm in boredom. It's like holding your breath—it starts out easy but gets harder and harder until it becomes impossible. You see, narrators are extremely verbal folk, so much so that they cannot bear silence for very long. Perhaps you know some people like that. But if there is anything more restless than a narrator who cannot narrate, it is a reader who cannot read, so we had best be getting on with it.

Narrator: Mr. Author, sir?

Author: Yes?

Narrator: I have been doing some thinking and, well—I guess I see your point. And I am sorry. So I was wondering, could I have my job back? What with this being the video generation and all, there is only a limited number of good jobs out there and I was really enjoying this one.

Author: All is forgiven. Just continue with the story.

"What's a conspiracy?" Percival asked.

Home on Derange

"The universe," said the Professor profoundly with a grand sweep of his hand. Percival wasn't much good at estimating ages, but he guessed the man with the disheveled hair, tweed jacket and plastic wrist bracelet was older than his father. "Oh, I used to think I had it all figured out. It was all so nice and neat, everything obeying the natural laws we were discovering. Every atom. Every galaxy. All very tidy. But then one day, I was preparing an experiment on the orbital patterns of asteroids. I had the computer generate some random numbers so I could assign the data to experimental and control groups. I was reviewing the numbers and everything seemed in order. That is, until I saw 1314! Now, don't ask me *how* I knew. I just knew. That number was not supposed to be there."

The Professor paused, waiting for Percival's acknowledgment of the significance of this. Percival, of course, had no idea what the man was talking about, but he sensed it was something important, so he offered, "Oh, yes, 1314."

"Exactly."

There was silence again, so Percival mulled it over in his mind for awhile. Finally, he said slowly, "1314. Sounds like trouble."

"Trouble! It's worse than trouble," said the Professor. "My whole world came unraveled that day. The universe isn't random after all—it's unpredictable. There's a huge difference. Science is based on the assumption that the history of the universe is a series of random events. These random events are subject to natural laws that have brought order out of chaos. It never bothered me before that the known natural laws don't explain all of the order we observe because I assumed it was attributable to natural laws as yet undiscovered. That's why people become scien-

The Life of Your Time

tists—to discover the laws we don't yet know. But 1314 showed me something new—something that was not governed by natural law and not random."

Again there was a pause. Percival prompted, "Something new?"

"Don't you see," said the Professor. "If there's order out there that's not natural, well—the implications are staggering! It means, it means . . ."

"It means there's a God?" asked Percival.

"Of course not!" said the Professor incredulously. "You look like an intelligent boy. You should know there's no such thing as God."

"Then what does it mean?"

"The blasted thing is organizing itself!" the Professor exclaimed.

"Huh?"

"I mean the universe is organizing itself. That's the conspiracy. I know it sounds crazy, but what other explanation is there? When you rule out everything else—the natural and the supernatural, it's the only alternative left. And for what reason? That's what I'd like to know. But I'll bet it's sinister. Natural disasters—that's just the beginning. Next thing you know, they'll be unionizing. Can you imagine what would happen if oxygen went on strike? Where would mankind be then? We would have to submit. No choice. All this time I thought I was in control. I was calling the shots. Now I find that it wasn't me manipulating the data, the data was manipulating me."

With that the Professor stopped talking and just stared blankly into space, looking about as glum as a person could. Percival had not really been able to follow much of the conversation at all, but he could see that the man was very distraught.

Then Percival got an idea. He walked across the street to the little drive-in and ordered two chocolate ice cream cones. Actually, he was ten cents short so he asked the girl at the window if she could make his soft-squeeze a little smaller. She smiled and filled both up to the same height. She told Percival that she had done it accidentally, and since it was her fault, she would not charge him the extra ten cents. He suspected she had done it on purpose, which was nice, so he thanked her kindly. He walked back across the street and offered one of them to the man who was still sitting there glumly staring at nothing in particular and said, "Ice cream always makes me feel better."

"I knew you were an intelligent boy."

They sat there together on the bench for awhile. Between licks, Percival asked him, "Have you told anyone about this? I mean, besides me."

"Try getting something like that published," he said. Since Percival had some recent experience getting something controversial published, he nodded sympathetically. "The university made me commit myself for a thirty-day psychiatric evaluation or risk losing my tenure." He nodded toward the hospital. "I'm not even sure I want to go back to teaching, though. What's the point?"

The sugar maples were at their peak of blazing color. Every so often a puff of wind would send newly-liberated leaves scurrying across the park and scraping along the sidewalk. Squirrels scampered busily under the oaks, though it was difficult to tell whether they were looking for acorns or just frolicking in the late afternoon sun.

"It's ironic," said the Professor. "Since I'm self-committed, I can get passes to go out whenever I want. I've thought about just not going back. But if I elope, I'm afraid they'll say that just proves I'm crazy and commit me for real."

Percival asked, "Do you feel good about yourself?"
"Not really."
"Me neither."
"Good ice cream, though," said the Professor.
"I guess we'd better enjoy it while we still can," said Percival with an ominous tone in his voice.
"Exactly," replied the Professor.

Blind Chance: Have you seen 1314?
Chaos: No, my lord. Why do you ask?
Blind Chance: I just find it rather odd that he's been keeping such a low profile lately. I was sure he'd be groveling for his old job by now.
Chaos: Are you going to give it to him?
Blind Chance: I've been considering it. After all, you have to admire the little pipsqueak's initiative. It was really rather humorous when you think about it—if it hadn't been such a reckless prank. He nearly gave us all away. You can't be that obvious with those intellectual types. They get suspicious. So, I had to teach 1314 a lesson. I probably should have reduced him to the Lowest Common Denominator, but he showed such promise. I thought a temporary firing would be sufficient. Now, though, I'm beginning to get concerned.
Chaos: I'm on the job, sire. I'll find him. No stone will be left unturned. You know how much I enjoy turning things over.
Blind Chance: Quite!

When Percival got home to his orderly house, everything looked as it did before. At the same time, though, it somehow seemed different. His mother was sitting on the sofa in the living room reading a magazine. He flopped down beside her with a big sigh and rested his head on her lap. "Bad day?" she asked.

Home on Derange

Percival nodded. His mother did not know a lot about little boys in general, but she did understand this one in particular. She did not press him for details, knowing that it was better to give him some space when he was in a reflective mood. Weckbaughs were not big on self-expression at times like these. If he wanted to talk about it, he would do so in his own time. Instead of prying, she hummed a little lullaby she used to sing to him when he was a baby and he closed his eyes.

Ann Weckbaugh used to love to sing. Growing up, she sang at school and she sang at church. She majored in music at college, starred in some local musical productions, and was even in a band because, as it turned out, people enjoyed listening to her sing.

Now it is a well known but little understood fact that music bypasses the normal perceptive faculties in human beings. Being formed in the heart of one, it penetrates directly to the heart of others. This was especially true in Ann's case. Her gift was such that she could lift people's hearts and make them soar or turn them inside out. She was considered a town treasure by the people of the community and they expected her to make a career of performing and become famous.

But somewhere along the way—she herself was not quite sure when or where—music ceased being what it once was for her. It was not, as many people gossiped, that she had married an older man who caused her to lose interest in life generally. Neither was it that after struggling for many years to conceive, the boy she gave birth to was not musically gifted, as Percival sometimes feared. Nor was it even, as those who knew her most intimately suspected, that she had always wanted a little girl of her own whom she could teach to sing—a dream that died on the day the doctor told her that was no longer a possibility.

The real reason was known to Ann alone, and she herself was only vaguely aware of it. She had simply run out of reasons to sing.

Chapter 5

Paradigms Lost

Ten miles up the interstate from Central City, an exit ramp led to a blacktop road that skirted the edge of the Kansas City suburbs. Five miles east, a dirt road wound its way up to the top of a bluff from the summit of which much of the metropolitan area could be seen. Although the road was abandoned and overgrown with weeds, Rick Callaway knew the place well. He and his friends frequently used this clandestine meeting place to throw parties when he was in high school.

Nearly two hundred feet below, the Missouri River rounded a bend downstream from the city. The limestone bluff upon which he stood was not straight down, but nearly so. Rick and his friends used to argue about whether you could jump out far enough to hit the river or would fall short and be smashed on the rocks at the edge of the water. It was purely a hypothetical argument since they all knew, even in their impaired conditions, that from that height it would not make much difference anyway. The outcome would be the same, though they agreed that the water landing would be superior by virtue of being less messy and making a great noise with the splash. Such are the morbid speculations of wild teenagers. But on this early October evening, Rick was not thinking about it in hypothetical terms anymore.

Rick had gotten by without needing to study very hard in high school, so he directed his energies to far less fruitful pursuits. Maybe the grades came too easily, he thought. Maybe he had too much time on his hands. Maybe his parents did not love him enough. Maybe he was trying to impress the wrong people. Maybe he was trying to escape the emptiness he felt inside. The rationalizations for his misfortunes were well rehearsed, though he did not have much of an audience for them any more.

He was certain that college would be better. Freedom—that was what he needed. Nobody to nag him about his hair or playing his stereo too loudly. Nobody to tell him what to do or when to go to bed. Freedom to live the good life, to have a good time, and do whatever he pleased—that was what life was all about. A few bad grades? No big deal. Those professors just did not like him. Academic probation? Who cares! He would pull it together next semester.

Physics was what really did him in. And to think he actually liked Professor Funkmeyer and thought the feeling was mutual. He was an interesting guy, Rick conceded. His academic credentials were impressive: department chair, three books and a long list of journal articles to his credit. Rick thought he was probably the most intelligent person he had ever known.

In the classroom, Professor Funkmeyer looked like the typical academician—turtleneck sweaters, tweed jackets with suede elbow patches and hair that always looked slightly in disarray. Outside of class, he was more, in Rick's terms, "laid back"—dressed in

Paradigms Lost

jeans, sweatshirts and sandals—and socialized regularly with the students at Dave's Tavern. (Rick had figured that Dave must be paying someone off because the underage students never got carded there.) The stories the Professor could tell were amazing. He had traveled all over the world and crossed paths with many famous people. And he must have been quite the rebel in his college days back in the '60s with all those stunts he pulled.

At the time, Rick thought it was "cool" that somebody like the Professor would hang out with the kids and not be such a stuffed shirt like his other teachers. Rick believed he had really connected with him. But now, for the first time, a realization flashed across his mind and he felt a tinge of sorrow for the man—that someone of his intelligence and academic achievements did not have anything better to do with his evenings than fraternize with students young enough to be his grandchildren and quaff down beers while reminiscing about the good old days. He had even heard a rumor that the poor soul had gone mad and had been committed to a mental institution. "What a waste," Rick said to himself. And those were probably the most sensible words he had uttered and the most compassionate feelings he had experienced toward another human being in a long, long time.

Instead of improving during that spring semester, as he had hoped, things had gone from bad to worse for Rick. He had been counting on a decent grade in Physics to keep his average above suspension level and felt certain that Professor Funkmeyer would, as Rick put it, "cut him some slack." After all, they were buddies. It had been a rude awakening when he got an "F" in that class. Very rude. That put his grades over the edge and, without fanfare, he was summarily kicked out of school.

The Life of Your Time

* * * * *

Approximately one hundred miles away in the same college town about which Rick was musing, Doug and Nancy were strolling along a walking path beside a small lake in a park not far from campus. Having just come from a pep rally, they were in high spirits. Doug was a tight end on the Missouri State University football team and there was a big game the following day.

As he walked along, though, Doug had something else on his mind besides the game. Now when it came to knocking opponents down or being pummeled by them, Doug was fearless. But when it came to matters of the heart and expressing them, his knees weakened, his stomach turned flip-flops and his tongue lagged far behind his feelings. At this particular moment, the distance between the heart and tongue seemed especially great.

Nancy caught Doug's eye in algebra class on her very first day of college. All she did was smile and say hello, but that was enough to capture his attention.

His first real opportunity to talk to her came a few weeks later when several of the students gathered in the student union to study on the night before their first exam. He had intended to ask her to the pep rally, but his knees wobbled and his stomach churned that night and he never quite got up the nerve. So he was pleased to see her when she showed up with several of her friends.

Afterward, he was headed back toward the athletic dorm with a couple of other players and passed by where Nancy and her friends were standing near the sidewalk. All she said was, "Good luck tomorrow!", so it must have been more the way she said it than what she said. It is also a bit of a mystery how, since it was spoken in the general direction of at least three players, Doug knew she was speaking to him, but he did. He slowed and told his buddies, "Hey, you guys go on. I'll catch up later."

The quarterback said, "Oh, we get it. You want to practice some of your moves before the big game."

The little wide receiver piped in, "Yo Doug! I'll show you some of my moves if you really want to see how it's done!"

"You morons," Doug yelled as he whizzed one of the toy footballs given out at the pep rally at them. He was not known for his throwing accuracy, however, and the ball sailed harmlessly between them. They high-fived each other and walked on laughing and making loud, sucking noises that were supposed to represent kisses.

"Don't pay any attention to those guys," Doug said sheepishly. "I think they've been playing without their helmets again."

Nancy laughed and said, "I'm sure it's just a 'guy' thing." And Doug appreciated the fact that she understood.

Soon they were walking along and talking about algebra and cafeteria food and how hard it was to find good parking spaces on campus. The park in which they eventually found themselves strolling was not technically part of the campus, but being adjacent, the students had colonized it and considered it their domain. Tonight, though, it was nearly deserted.

Away from the lights and noise of Friday night college life, the conversation lagged. Doug felt more than a little uncomfortable during the long moments of silence. He wanted to say something, but was not quite sure what it was. Even if he had known what he wanted to say, he did not know if he could find the right words.

At one end of the lake was a small fishing dock where they stopped and gazed out over the water. Doug finally managed to say, "My grandfather taught me to fish on a dock like this one."

He immediately wanted to kick himself for saying it. Here he was—alone with this beautiful girl who made his heart pound every time he got near her and he brings up fishing and everyone knows most girls hate fishing and she's going to think he's just another dumb athlete who can't think about anything except sports and hormones and . . .

"Tell me about him," said Nancy.

"My grandfather—he's a great man," said Doug, relieved that she had not recoiled at the thought of fish and slimy worms. "A colonel in the Air Force. Retired now. Highly decorated. Got shot down in Vietnam and spent eighteen months in a POW camp, but lived to tell about it."

There was no one Doug Martin admired more than his grandfather. Of course he loved his father, and while there was all the normal baggage that often gets between fathers and sons, he had a good relationship with him. But the Colonel was bigger than life.

Since the Colonel moved frequently and was often stationed in distant places, Doug as a young child saw him only occasionally. But once Adrian Martin retired and settled down in Central City to be near his family, he had spent much time with Doug. And fishing was not all his grandfather taught him. Doug learned that being a true hero was not about fighting battles, but being a man of faith and convictions and integrity and sacrificing for others. The lad listened well and took the advice to heart. Although he was not quite twenty years old, Doug could already see the difference it had made in his life.

Many of his classmates had made different choices in high school and college. He thought of Rick and how they had been fast friends from junior high on. But when Rick started hanging out with a different crowd, they drifted apart. Doug had tried to warn him he was headed for trouble, but Rick would not listen. Watching his downhill slide had been painful. Doug must have been trying to block it out of his memory as he had not even thought about Rick much at all since he dropped out of college. Funny that he should pop into his mind at this particular moment. "I really ought to call him," Doug thought and made a mental note to do so. But at the moment, he had something more urgent on his mind.

* * * * *

Rick would never forget that May night when he broke the bad news about his grades to his parents. It was the worst night of his life—worse even than when Jerry left home, a night he only vaguely recalled.

Jerry, the oldest. Jerry, the favorite son. Jerry, the perpetually unrecalled memory that locked the Callaway household in a permanent state of amnesia. Rick was barely old enough to remember his brother who was sixteen years his senior—a difference that had always made Rick suspect his arrival into the world had not been planned. He had even stronger suspicions that it had not been welcomed.

His mother Sylvia had always doted on Jerry, which was short for Jeremiah. She lavished attention upon him and bought him everything she imagined he could want.

The Life of Your Time

Joseph, in his role as father, was considerably more reserved. An accountant by trade and temperament, he nevertheless held out high hopes for the boy and planned for Jerry to follow in his footsteps. Someday they would have a rewarding and fulfilling relationship as business partners.

What neither Sylvia nor Joseph expected was that Jerry would not care for any of these things—neither toys nor money nor business success. He was a dreamer, whose chief pleasure in life was music. Although he was one of those multi-talented people to whom nearly everything seemed to come easily, none of it seemed very fulfilling save music, which alone provided some satisfaction by allowing him to express the lack of fulfillment he experienced in other areas of his life.

Sylvia and Joseph saw this too late. Or, perhaps to put it more precisely, they never saw Jerry withdrawing from them at all. Their blindness was such that by the time the day came and angry words were exchanged, what was no more than the next logical step in a process of estrangement to Jerry was the shock of many lifetimes to his parents: Jerry dropped out of college and left home at the age of twenty-two. They had not heard from him since.

That was fourteen years ago and life at the Callaways had never been the same. A stifling cloud hung over their lives, an unrelenting rainy season that never dried out and was never followed by the sun, because a change of season requires a passage of time or of something beyond time. But to the Callaways, life had become one big "now" as all meaningful references to the past were meticulously expunged, lest they be reminded of the pain that existed there. And because there was no past, there could be no future—no hope to look forward to and no process to get them there. All that was left was existence.

The only reference Rick could remember in the ensuing fourteen years was the one he most wished that he could forget. It came on the day he got his report card and expulsion notice and that in itself had not been a good way to start his morning.

At first, he was so shocked himself that he could scarcely believe it. Then he began searching for an escape clause. He thought there surely must be an appeal process as he was the kind of person who always managed to find a way out.

"A way out," he thought to himself as he sat there in the darkness on the bluff. "That's what I need right now—a way out."

But when he called the university from a payphone that afternoon, he found that it would be at least a year before he could reapply. Even then, he would have to show proof of academic achievement at a junior college or equivalent.

He spent the rest of the afternoon mustering up the courage to tell his parents. "Maybe they won't take it too badly," he thought. "After all, they never seemed to think my future looked too promising anyway."

After a couple of beers and some vigorous psychological gymnastics, he had himself half convinced that he might even enjoy telling them. He would savor the looks on their faces as sweet revenge for their shabby treatment of him.

When he told them, though, his mother immediately ruined his enjoyment by crying. But he could handle that. After all, she cried at soap operas.

It was Joseph Callaway, CPA, who really got to Rick. He got up out of his chair and crossed over to where Rick was sitting. Momentarily, Rick thought his father intended to strike him. But Joseph's

The Life of Your Time

response was not a blow struck in the heat of anger, rather an icy dagger calculated to pierce his heart: "I wish to God it had been you who left instead of Jerry." That said, Joseph turned and strode out of the room, leaving Rick stunned and silent.

There it was, out in the open. Rick's long-unspoken fear had been uttered. Like a sorcerer's secret incantation, his father's words roused a sleeping dragon within him. This dragon had remained cloistered away in the deep dark recesses of his mind since childhood and Rick was quite willing to let it remain so. But now that it was awakened, only two choices remained: slay it or be devoured.

So far, the dragon was getting much the better of the struggle and other circumstances in his life were not helping. His so-called friends, upon learning that he had been dismissed from college, labeled him a loser and quit socializing with him. His pseudo-girlfriend Cindy informed him she did not want to see him anymore—ever. Joseph and Sylvia barely spoke to him and were only letting him live at home long enough to make arrangements to move out. That would be none too soon for Rick, because he could not bear his father's "I knew you would never amount to anything" looks. To make matters worse, everyone his age was back at school and he felt very alone.

Rick had taken some odd jobs over the summer before getting full-time work at a local service station. The irony was not lost on him that he had once hoped to be a mechanical engineer and he was now just a mechanic. And not much of one at that. Since he was not certified, he mostly did menial tasks at the beck and call of the real mechanics. At six bucks an hour and with dim prospects for advancement, his dreams of freedom and the good life now seemed permanently out of reach.

Paradigms Lost

He started to curse everyone in his life again for driving him to this point, but stopped himself. Enough excuses, he thought. It was pointless to blame his parents or Cindy or his ex-friends or his teachers. Deep down, he had known all along that he alone was responsible for messing up his own life. That was far worse. Mr. Wimbley, had he been present, would probably have observed that Rick felt very bad about himself—so bad, in fact, that he was considering very drastic solutions to those bad feelings.

* * * * *

Meanwhile, in Central City, Percival was getting ready for bed. Having already said his "goodnights," he happened to look out of his bedroom window. Their home was on the south edge of Central City and Percival's bedroom faced an open field in the opposite direction from Kansas City twelve miles up the interstate. On a clear, moonless night like this one, with the light off in his room, he could see all but the faintest stars in the southern sky. As he gazed into the cosmos, a seemingly insignificant bit of iron that had careened around the solar system for an untold number of orbits met with a sudden dazzling demise as it struck the earth's atmosphere.

As Percival witnessed the shooting star streaking across the darkling sky, it occurred to him that it was the saddest event he had ever witnessed. His eyes burned, but only a little. The sadness he felt was beyond tears. In his nearly twelve years of life on this tiny, remote planet, he had never felt more alone and unimportant in this hostile, dog-eat-dog universe.

Percival climbed into bed, pulled the covers over his head and drifted off into a dreamscape haunted by thin mustaches and old English teachers. Exhausted

The Life of Your Time

as he was, however, he could not later recall whether the old English teachers were actually wearing the thin mustaches.

* * * * *

Rick turned up the collar of his leather jacket and zipped it all the way. The air was crisp now that the sun had gone down, but Rick was sweating and that gave him a chill. He was sober tonight—for a change. He wanted to do some serious thinking and a clear head helped.

As Rick peered down at the black water, he tried to fathom its depths. Although he could not see his reflection in the water, he could clearly make out the color of his heart in the darkness. He hated what he saw. Longing to put an end to the pain, he speculated on whether the comforting forgetfulness of oblivion lay beneath the surface of the water. He could think of only one way to find out for sure.

"If only . . . ," he said to himself. "If only what? If only a person could have a second chance at life. If only there was a reason to keep on trying. If only I knew that someone in this whole stinkin' universe gave a rip about me. If only . . . if You are out there, please let me know. I can't take it anymore."

At that precise moment, the same shooting star Percival had just seen flashed across the sky. And although Professor Funkmeyer would have scoffed at Rick's reaction and written the coincidence off as iron molecules conspiring to delude a troubled teen, Rick interpreted the phenomenon differently. He dropped to his knees and began making many promises to the God of Second Chances.

* * * * *

"Your grandfather sounds like a special person," said Nancy. "I'd like to meet him sometime."

Her words startled Doug out of his reverie, but he thought the part about wanting to meet his grandfather was a very encouraging sign. "He'll be at the game tomorrow. Maybe you can meet him then."

As Nancy and Doug stood on the end of the dock, staring up at the stars, Nancy said, "It's a beautiful night, isn't it?"

Doug wanted to say something profound, but all that came out of his mouth was "Yep." And that did not seem adequate.

Suddenly, a shooting star streaked across the sky—yes, the very same one.

"That was incredible!" Nancy exclaimed.

"Not as incredible as you are," said Doug. It was a pretty good line for someone to whom such things did not come easily—probably because he meant it.

They turned to face each other and then they kissed. In all the years to come, Doug and Nancy would always remember this as the precise moment when they fell in love.

Chapter 6

Computer Bugs and Hard Drive Crashes

Although it was after 10:00 p.m. when Nancy got back to the dorm, she called her sister Kate to tell her the exciting news. Even though Kate was five years older, the Chandler sisters had always been close and never kept any secrets from one another—at least not until that night. Nancy just bubbled as she talked about Doug and how he was starting on the football team this year even though he was only a sophomore and how much they had in common and how they had taken a walk by the lake and how he told her she was incredible.

"An athlete," Kate moaned to herself. "Great." She started to tell Nancy that she was making a huge mistake, but thought better of it. "Let her enjoy life while she can," she thought. "Reality sets in soon enough."

Kate and Terry had been happy once, but that seemed like a thousand years ago. She could remember a time when she felt the same romantic excitement just being around him and how he cherished her. But it was a memory that seemed to fade a bit more each day. Like an old newspaper photo, the recollection captured a moment in time, now gone, and the image itself was yellowed and crumbling.

Terry had built his own separate life and most of it did not include her. He worked long hours, and when he was not working, he golfed or attended ball games with his friends. Even when he was at home, he took every opportunity to point out that she was failing to live up to his expectations. He even had the audacity to wonder why she did not just melt in his arms every time he walked in the door. The only passion she had in her life was her art, and that was a poor substitute for love.

"I'm happy for you, Sis," Kate said flatly, trying to keep her voice steady. That was not easy because she had been crying when the phone rang. Even though she had grown resentfully accustomed to Terry's long work hours, he was way past his normally late coming-home time. "Where is he?" she wondered, but was afraid she did not want to know the answer.

"Are you okay?" asked Nancy.

Kate started to tell Nancy the whole truth about her troubled marriage. Nancy was a great listener and Kate had always been able to confide in her. It was wonderful to have grown up with someone to talk out her problems with, but she could not bring herself to broach this topic. In fact, there was a level at which she did not want to admit it to herself. She felt as if saying it aloud would give her fear a reality that she did not want it to have. To fail at marriage was like failing at life, she thought. And she was determined not to fail—not insofar as it depended on her. So she hoped a desperate hope that the ebb tide of their love would swell again. "I think we've just got a bad connection," she said. "I'd better go before we get cut off."

Computer Bugs and Hard Drive Crashes

* * * * *

The problems that started at the phone company's computer with the placing of Nancy's call are highly technical, but they are relevant to the story in a roundabout way. It was not the overall number of calls, because the total usage at that hour was low. Perhaps it was more the particular combination of calls that caused a switching error that led to a minute power surge that corrupted a data field. Or it might have been one of those things that just happen and nobody ever really knows why.

Whatever the reason, the computer began shutting down numbers off the grid automatically. Nancy and Kate were not even aware of a problem except that there was an unusual amount of static on the line and perhaps that is why Nancy did not detect more readily the stress in her sister's voice. But within thirty minutes, several hundred people in various parts of the state were without telephone service.

Narrator: Aren't you going to tell the reader what the last four digits of Kate's phone number were?
Author: I don't think I need to. This reader seems very perceptive and will probably figure it out without being told.
Narrator: You are the boss. Whatever you say.

On the other side of Central City, Terry McKinzie was where he knew he should not be. It was not so much the place. He had been in bars lots of times. It was more the situation—sitting in a dimly lit corner with a woman who was not his wife.

Marla Roberts, a recent college graduate, had come to the radio station three months ago. She worked in sales and promotions, but air time did not seem to be all she was selling nor the station all she was promoting. Marla was as ambitious as she was good looking and she was the type who would use her assets to the fullest possible advantage to get what she wanted.

Terry willed himself to stop looking nervously around the room. After all, they were co-workers. If anyone recognized him, they were just a couple of workaholics discussing business after hours. That was plausible, even if it was not the truth.

In reality, business was the last thing on Terry's mind at that moment. He was only paying enough attention to Marla's suggestions for improving the station to know when to nod and say, "That's a great idea," even though he had not given them an ounce of consideration. What was really occupying his thoughts were the signals she had been sending. He was a good-looking guy and he had seen them before. They were unmistakable.

But acting on them was another matter. Terry and Kate had been high-school sweethearts and he used to think he was the luckiest guy in the world. To his way of thinking, he never had a reason to be unfaithful before.

Their marriage, however, had begun to feel like a prison to him. Kate had become so unresponsive. All she seemed to care about was her art. If she wanted to fritter away her time drawing and painting, fine with him. But she could at least have dinner on the table when he got home from work. And she was always badgering him to take her to museums and art shows, which seemed an unfair expectation to him since he did not make her accompany him to ball games or force her to go golfing when he went with his buddies. He thought, "What does she expect from me anyway?"

Computer Bugs and Hard Drive Crashes

The bass beat of the dance tune thumped in the background as Terry sipped his beer. He half-listened as Marla related her suggestions for a new promotional concept. Terry, however, was far more intent on a proposition than a proposal. He studied her face and noted how her short dark hair accentuated her lips which always seemed to hint at pouting even when she was smiling. His eyes wandered down to her outfit. "Professional," he thought. "But provocative. Just like everything else about her."

When Marla seemed to be finished talking, Terry said, "Super ideas, Marla," though for all the attention he was paying she could have been talking for the last hour about being abducted by extraterrestrials. "Put together a written proposal and I'll recommend it to Bob."

"Bob" was Robert R. Froerking, the station owner, and only Terry, of all the station employees, called him Bob. Mr. Froerking was an old friend of Terry's family. In his earlier days, he was known as "Railroad" Froerking for his initials R.R. and the nickname fit his reputed business style. In his golden years, though, he had mellowed considerably. Whether this was due to the fact that he had reached a position of wealth and influence that no longer required a "get off the tracks I'm coming through" approach or the accumulated wisdom of a lifetime led him to be more reflective is hard to say.

Whatever the reason, Mr. Froerking had encouraged Terry's interest in broadcast media and taken him under his wing. Terry was only two years out of college when Froerking named him general manager of his adult contemporary station in Central City. Terry was grateful. Who wouldn't be? A lot of his college classmates were still late night disc jockeys. Froerking had jump-started his career, shared a wealth of experience with him, and introduced him to many influential people in the industry—heady stuff for a twenty-four-year-old. Of course he was grateful to Froerking. But in Terry's mind, that did not mean it had to be forever.

The moment of decision came sooner than expected when Marla said, "Why don't we go work on the proposal right now—at my place?"

He had to admit she was smooth. An open invitation had been issued, but it was safely ambiguous. She would keep her options open until the last possible second. Terry's two options, though, were about to be reduced to one depending on what he decided to do in the next moment. He gripped the beer glass tightly to keep his hands from shaking, knowing that one step toward the door with her would mean crossing a bridge of no return.

He thought about Kate and how she would take it. She would be hurt, he rationalized, but she would survive. They had some great times together. There was no denying that. But they were two different people. She was just not meeting his needs anymore. Life was too short to waste precious time on a doomed relationship. It would be better for both of them to just get on with their lives.

All at once he followed her, like the proverbial ox going to the slaughter. He crossed the bridge and set it on fire behind him as they exited the night club.

Whatever it was that caught Terry's toe, he did not see it. One moment he was walking on the sidewalk to the parking lot with Marla and the next he was flying through the air. In his slightly inebriated condition, his efforts to regain his balance or even break his fall were in vain. He landed hard on the curb with his face.

Computer Bugs and Hard Drive Crashes

* * * * *

Midnight was approaching when the phone rang at the Weckbaugh home.

"George? It's Rico."

"Frederico?" said George groggily. "What's up? Don't tell me that Kelsing Equipment program blew up again. I'll be right down."

"George, I don't know anything about any Kelsing Equipment program. I left BBI eight months ago, remember?"

"Oh, yes. Right. You're at the phone company now." George yawned. "Are you okay?"

"I'm okay at least until morning," said Frederico. "Sorry to call you in the middle of the night but, man, I got big problems here and I don't know what to do. In fact, I'm lucky I got through at all. That's why I called you. You taught me everything I know about troubleshooting."

"You *do* have problems then," said George.

Frederico managed a half-hearted laugh. "You got that right."

"I'm flattered that you would think to call me," said George, "but I don't know anything about your system."

"Maybe that's a good thing," said Frederico. "I do know it and I'm fresh out of ideas. Maybe if I had a couple of weeks, I could figure it out. But if I can't patch something together by business hours tomorrow . . . well, I've just heard that if commercial service gets interrupted during peak hours, heads are liable to roll."

So George sat there in his pajamas and bathrobe with only a nightlight on and talked to his former colleague about a computer system he knew nothing about. "Well, let's start with the facts. What do you know for certain? Have you had any luck trying to isolate the effect?"

"I remember the drill," said Frederico. "But that's part of the problem. I don't see any kind of pattern. I'm losing numbers out of service, but it seems like it's just happening at random."

"Rico, you know computers don't behave randomly," said George. "They just do what they're programmed to do."

"I know. But you should see this thing."

"So what are you looking at?" asked George.

"The diagnostic monitor," said Frederico staring at the pulsating, multicolored screen. "But it's no help. Everything shows normal except that five hundred numbers are going out of service every hour."

"Well, maybe we'd better look somewhere else," said George.

"What do you mean?"

"Well, if there's nothing physically wrong with the lines internally . . ."

"I don't know that for sure," Frederico interrupted. "Something must be wrong with them or they wouldn't be showing up out of service."

"But just assume your diagnostics are correct and that the numbers are fine," said George. "Let's think bigger—system wide."

"You've lost me," said Frederico, baffled.

"Well, what would turn a number off and on?"

"You mean, like a work order?"

"I don't know," said George. "You tell me."

"But that's a different system."

"They interface, don't they?"

"Yeah, but the service reps only work nine to five. They wouldn't be putting in work orders this time of night to turn off numbers."

"But it's a place to start," said George. "Can you get in?"

"Yeah, hang on," said Frederico and then after a bit, "Okay, I'm in." He scanned the program quickly as it was fairly short and straightforward. "I'm looking. I don't see anything, but I can't tell for sure without going through line by line and I don't have time for that."

"What else would take a working number out of service?"

"Man, I don't know!" said Frederico, his frustration starting to get the better of him. "Maybe they didn't pay their bills." He said it as a joke, but as soon as he said it, something clicked (in his head, not the phone).

"Rico?" George said after a long pause.

"Hang on George. I'm checking something." A minute or so went by and then Rico said, "Okay, I'm looking at the billing routine." This was a considerably longer and more complex program, so it took him several minutes to even scroll down through it. "This is crazy. I really should be looking at the switching program. Nothing's jumping out at me. It would take days to go through all this."

"Can you pull up some of the actual customer bills?" asked George.

"What for?"

"Just fishing."

"Okay, okay. Give me a second," said Frederico. "All right, they're running. Here's one—looks all right. Here's another—all right. All right. All right. Whoa! Look at that!"

"What?"

"A final past-due notice."

"What about it?"

"Where the date is supposed to be—it's just a string of numbers," said Frederico. "I wonder . . . Let me check something . . . Bingo! That's one of the out-of-service numbers! Maybe we're on to something." He toggled back over to the billing program code. "Look at that little devil! The payment date field lost its formatting. It's just reading numbers as text. Every time it processes one of those unformatted payment dates, it's thinking 'no payment' and automatically taking the number out of service. Hey, Joe! Come in here. I got it! Call Charlie and tell him to get his carcass out of bed and get down here pronto! His billing program is blowing up. While you're at it, call Jesse. Hey, I don't care if she goes ballistic. She knows that program, too. Tell her she can have Thanksgiving weekend off like she wanted if she's here in thirty minutes. Oh yeah, George? You still there?"

"Yes, Rico."

"Man, you really saved my neck tonight!"

"Hey, you came up with the answers," said George. "All I did was ask a couple of questions."

"But you asked the right questions. That's the main thing. I gotta split. Six hours isn't much time, but I think we can make it now that we know what the problem is. Thanks man. I owe you—again."

"Anytime Rico. Keep in touch." As he hung up the phone, George chuckled to himself, "Like I always say, they just do what they're programmed to do."

Rico and his team sprang into action. The formatting error was simple to fix and though they had to write a new routine to identify and correct the billing errors, it also was accomplished fairly quickly since it was all internal—none had actually been mailed or even printed. By sunup the next day, service had been restored to all their customers, the vast majority of whom were unaware their service had been interrupted. Everything turned out well, though no one ever got around to figuring out how the date field lost its formatting.

* * * * *

The needle that applied the local anesthetic stung Terry's swollen chin like a hornet and he winced. Searing pain and the sight of his own blood had gone a long way toward sobering him up, an effect he was regretting at present.

He glanced at the clock on the treatment room wall and cursed to himself. He had no idea the hour was so late. He began rehearsing in his mind what he was going to tell Kate, though it was difficult to think clearly with what was probably a mild concussion while the emergency room physician jabbed needles into his skin.

Terry was glad that Marla had volunteered to call Kate. For one thing, he would not have known what to say. Moreover, it would look less suspicious that way—like he had nothing to hide. "It was all very innocent," he thought. "Just business. That's all. Business. Yeah, right. Like she's really going to buy that."

The doctor was just tying off the last stitch when Kate arrived at the hospital. The look on her face hurt Terry worse than the fall and treatment combined. It took five stitches to patch him up and the cut would leave a noticeable scar on his handsome chin. But this cut was only skin deep. The deeper wounds would be more difficult to heal.

Marla played the innocent co-worker to the hilt—to the point where Terry even began to wonder if he had been imagining things. But deep down he knew differently.

The Life of Your Time

Kate drove Terry home in silence—a silence that seemed to convict him. He knew full well he ought to say something, but every excuse that came to his mind would probably have made the situation worse. So he shut his eyes and hoped the trip would soon be over. Although it was only a couple of miles, the drive seemed to take a very long time.

Perhaps it is just a coincidence, or perhaps not, that Terry was the Clock Man—the one who originally asked Percival what time it was in the beginning. Strangely enough, he himself had not given the incident another moment's thought.

Chapter 7

Screen Savor

George sat in his chair for a long time after he hung up the phone, his own last words to Frederico echoing in his ears. He had a vague uneasiness in his mind that he could not quite explain. Maybe he was disoriented from being awakened in the middle of the night, he thought. But this was not the first time he had gotten such a call. It happened at least two or three times a year that some computer glitch could not wait until morning, though always before it had at least been his own company—Bailey Brothers, Inc.—that called.

Jonathan and Bradley Bailey founded the company some thirty years earlier to support small businesses that could not afford to hire their own staff for accounting and billing services. It had been modestly successful in its own right, but where they really started making money was buying out clients in whom they saw potential. They quickly diversified, which helped them remain strong during a lot of ups and downs in particular sectors of the economy. Known throughout the region as shrewd businessmen, the Bailey brothers became very wealthy men.

The Life of Your Time

George Weckbaugh had gotten in on the ground floor of BBI back when computers were just emerging as a dominant factor in business technology. In fact, with his intelligence and longevity, George could have long since become vice president of information systems except for one insurmountable problem—he had absolutely no aptitude or interest in management. This attribute (or lack thereof) had long posed a dilemma for the company. He could not be promoted because any higher position would have required him to supervise people, which he steadfastly refused to do. Therefore, as the years went by, he found himself being supervised by people who were increasingly his junior.

You might think that someone in George's situation would be in serious jeopardy of being re-engineered out of a job, and in a lot of companies that would certainly have been the case. But George had two factors working in his favor. First and foremost was that the Bailey brothers had really liked him. While some people considered them ruthless (what shrewdness sometimes looks like from the receiving end), they were loyal to the long-term employees who helped build the company. Although the elder Bailey had died some years ago and Bradley was semi-retired, Jonathan Junior, who was now chief executive officer, knew that George was on the "untouchable" list—at least as long as his Uncle Bradley was alive. Jonathan Junior was not the same caliber man his father was, but at least he had enough sense to know which side his bread was buttered on. And it worked out well for George because even though he had not had a raise in years, he at least got a nice bonus at Christmas.

The second reason had to do with another Bailey brothers' characteristic—they were sticklers for details. They were not just interested in last quarter's earnings, they wanted to know what that company had done in the last quarter century, if that information was available. This made the ability to recover archived data a premium in the company. In the early years, that had meant transcribing vast amounts of handwritten records onto their computer system, while in more recent years most of the data was converted electronically.

That is where a detail-oriented man like George fit in. While the younger guys could program circles around him in the new languages (though George's routines usually ran right the first time, saving lots of time in de-bugging later), George had hands-on experience with a variety of systems that had become obsolete before some of them were even born. Since many of the small businesses BBI acquired or had as clients used these older systems, there was an ongoing demand for George's services.

Therefore, George was given an office by himself in the basement (some of the younger programmers nicknamed it "the Dungeon") because it was the only place big enough—and out of the way enough—to house all of the old and unsightly computer junk used to recover the archived data. Now even for a total computer nerd, this might seem a bit extreme. George got all of the ignoble jobs that the other technicians hated, while all the glamorous jobs went to the young hotshots trying to make names for themselves. This setup obviously would not have been for everyone, but it suited George in an odd sort of way and he had been reasonably happy at BBI over the years.

The impression that George was totally isolated in "the Dungeon" would be erroneous, because George had a reputation among the veterans as the best troubleshooter in information systems. Many of them had nearly come to ruin over some programming bug only to have George rescue them. Admitting they needed help from the over-the-hill guy in the basement was a rather humbling experience for some of the upstarts. At least one guy had even gotten fired rather than ask.

George enjoyed this aspect of his job like some people enjoy brain teasers and crossword puzzles. The greater the challenge, the more satisfaction he got out of it. Having worked with many different software languages and hardware systems over the years, he had gained a deep appreciation of the structure of computer logic in much the same way as learning foreign languages helps a person to better understand the nature of language itself—that is, distinguishing the universal characteristics of communication from those which are unique to each language.

Although George found problem-solving highly satisfying, he was never one to gloat over his successes and was always quick to credit his colleagues. This was not just false humility because, in a way, it was true. Since he was not the resident expert in any of the newer systems, he frequently had to rely on others. It was often during the course of George's questions that the answer presented itself and, in many cases, the person ended up solving his or her own problem. The glory hogs were quick to usurp all the credit for themselves, but the more circumspect realized they would not have gotten the right answer, or gotten it as quickly, if not for the right question. When credit was unavoidable, George was always fond of saying, "They just do what they're programmed to do," as if it were all the machine's doing and none of his own.

Frederico Hernandez was one who had come to appreciate George's assistance. When he was first hired, his co-workers had not gone out of their way to be friendly to him. Some had even gone as far as insinuating (behind his back, of course) that his hiring and advancement were because he was Hispanic rather than because of merit. This was untrue. Although his parents had immigrated from Mexico, Frederico was born in the U.S. And, while he did speak Spanish, he considered English his native language. He had been hired not as part of a quota, but upon the recommendation of his departmental advisor to the BBI recruiter that he was the top graduate in computer science that year.

Frederico had been given an extremely tough assignment right out of training and he half suspected that it might have been because his supervisor wanted him to fail. But he took it as a challenge, understanding that if he was going to get ahead, he was going to have to work harder than everybody else. This was an opportunity to show what he could do.

Frederico's optimism soon turned to disillusionment, however, when he realized he was in over his head. He began to doubt himself and wonder if what his co-workers thought about him were true. One of the more sympathetic among them suggested that he talk to George. Frederico had heard of George and wondered, "Who is this dude in the basement? Like Dr. Frankenstein or something?"

But desperate times call for desperate measures, so one afternoon he ventured into the Dungeon and asked George for help. They worked on into the evening and, by the time they went home, Frederico had the outline of a solution and he knew he could fill in the rest.

That day was a turning point for Frederico, because he not only had the brains to succeed, he also had a rare blend of confidence and humility—confidence that helped him quickly to be named a project director and humility enough to ask for help when he needed it without feeling threatened. He had gone a long way at BBI before the phone company lured him away with a big salary, though he never forgot where he came from. He had even offered George a job, but George turned him down as Frederico knew he would. Probably the closest Frederico would ever come to repaying him for his kindness was the fact that George was the first person he thought of to call in the middle of the night when he was in a jam.

George would come to appreciate that more in future times, but at that moment he was troubled. The fact that he did not know why heightened his sense of uneasiness. True, he had been unusually busy at work in the past several weeks on a problem that seemed insoluble. BBI had just acquired Johnson Supply, a cleaning supply wholesaler and, as usual, the company wanted to convert as much of the data as possible. The executives were particularly interested in the historical accounts receivable so they could document which customers and which product lines had been most lucrative over time. The problem was that the system was a veritable antique by computer standards and the company that wrote the software had been acquired three times before the software was discontinued.

George had concluded that it was a pretty mediocre piece of work even in its day. He could not make heads or tails of the file architecture and had spent most of one morning on the phone trying to track down someone somewhere in the world who knew anything at all about it. Finally, he had found a woman in Boston who seemed to know what she was talking about and agreed to help—for a fee of course, since the company no longer supported that product.

They talked on the phone two to three times a week and she was pleasant to talk to—which one would expect for $150-an-hour consulting fee. However, her help was limited by the fact that she had not worked on it on a daily basis for over eight years.

Thus, the process of extracting the data was slow and difficult. Within about three weeks George had pried just about all the knowledge out of her he was going to get. In fact, she was starting to ask more questions than he was. George's supervisor had been furious when he mentioned that he had shared information with her about how he had gotten to some of the data. "Weckbaugh! There's something you're not understanding here. We pay her the big bucks and she gives us information—not the other way around!" A lesser man would have told that supervisor—who was about half his age—that he had socks older than he was, but the thought never even occurred to George.

While George was able to extract most of the information out of the old system, what he most wanted— the accounts receivable records—eluded him. So he placed one more call to the woman in Boston.

"I'm afraid I can't help you on that one, George."

"Why not?"

"You can't get to it," she said.

"What do you mean?" he said. "It's got to be there somewhere."

"It is there, but like I said, you can't get to it. Not the way you want it. The billing data all reside in the billing routine. There's no way to associate it back to the client record."

"That doesn't make any sense," said George. "How did they bill their customers and pay their own bills?"

"There is an internal linking routine, but as it moves through the receivable or payable process, the data are aggregated. All that was physically associated with the client record after that was the balance."

"That must have been fun to audit."

"Frankly, it did prove to be a big flaw in the system," she said. "The updated version handled it differently."

"So there's no way to link the bills back to the client."

"The link was designed to work in only one direction. I knew the guy who wrote this part of the program and he never had any luck retrieving it, if that tells you anything. I wouldn't waste my time trying."

"But I get paid to waste my time trying," said George.

She laughed. "You'd better hope for a miracle then, because that's the only way to do what you want to do."

After two more weeks of working almost exclusively on this project, he was more than ready to agree with her. He tried everything he could think of but all he came up with were blank screens or error messages. He had already conceded in his mind, though not to his boss, that it was a lost cause. He had been saying to himself for at least four days, "I'll just try this one last thing. . . ," but he kept on thinking of one more thing.

Then, with no warning, something happened. George had not even been in the room at the time. He had gone upstairs to get a cup of coffee and stopped to chat with one of the other analysts about some recurring coding errors. He had started the extraction program running for what seemed like the thousandth time before he left and when he got back, there on the screen was all the information he had been trying so hard to get! Normally, he would have felt like celebrating—going to the donut shop and eating a jelly belly or something daring like that—but this had been such a nasty little program that he mainly felt relieved. He carefully downloaded it onto his workstation from the mainframe and made a backup of the program and the data. After all that effort, he did not want to take any chances.

He called his supervisor and told him the good news. "It's about time," his supervisor said. "The suits have been all over my back about that information. Don't worry about running it in report form. Just shoot it over to me and I'll package it (translated, "I'll make it pretty and put my name on it so I'll get credit for it.") You just get cracking on the Jenkins project. We're already behind schedule." After that, George had felt even less like celebrating. Drained, he went home early that day.

But now, sitting there in the middle of the night, this project kept bugging him and he could not understand why. After all, it had worked. It *had* worked.

He finally went back to bed. Although he dozed some, he never really got back into a restful sleep.

* * * * *

George rose early on Saturday. Sometime during the night, he had decided to go to the office for awhile. He did not normally work on weekends, reserving that time for his family. But on this day, he felt an overwhelming compulsion to go.

It was quiet at BBI on Saturdays, almost strangely so. As soon as he got to the Dungeon, he checked the Johnson Supply data file. He was half afraid that he had just dreamed he had gotten it and that it would not really be there, but it was.

Then, out of curiosity, he checked the extraction program, trying to figure out what it was that was bothering him. He studied the code line by line, reconstructing his logic. He had tried so many different approaches that he had forgotten what he had done on this particular one. Now, as he analyzed it carefully, he began to experience a sinking sensation in the pit of his stomach as he realized, "This never should have worked!"

George pressed the series of keystrokes which set the program running. Immediately, it returned an error message. He was right. It should never have worked.

He ran it again and got the same error message. He shoved in the backup disk and loaded it, just to make sure. It was, indeed, the same program. He ran it—error. He executed the system maintenance program to search for bad files or other problems, but everything checked out okay. Then he ran the extraction program again—error.

George stared at the screen in disbelief. A fuzzy thinker might have dismissed the incident as a fluke, but George was not a fuzzy thinker. His whole world view revolved around the assumption that things do what they are programmed to do—from computers to galaxies. Natural laws determine how the world unfolds like programs run computers. But here was something new—a category of phenomena that was not programmed.

For a moment, he considered the possibility that the computer had somehow learned what it was that George wanted and retrieved it for him since he was not getting it on his own. He knew that scientists all over the world were using computers to create artificial intelligence, trying to get them to think and learn. In some respects, they had achieved some remarkable successes. George himself had long since come to recognize that every complex machine had its own "temperament." But this was really just an anthropomorphism. As advanced as the technology had become, computers were, in the final analysis, simply really fast calculating machines. They would never be able to think creatively or have a will or emotions. In these respects, even a young child would always be a quantum step ahead of even the most sophisticated supercomputer.

But if he dismissed the notion that the computer had done something on its own that it was not programmed to do, that implied something even more profound. His familiar surroundings in the Dungeon seemed suddenly eerie. For a moment, he had a sensation that he was not alone. While he did not actually run out of the building, anyone who had seen him would have thought he was in a terrible hurry.

Although George was shaken, he at least had the presence of mind to notice that he was running low on gas. He pulled into the gas station that was located at the top of the entrance ramp to the interstate. He filled his tank, went inside to pay and decided a cup of coffee might help settle his nerves.

Rick Callaway did not normally work the register, but the girl who was scheduled called in sick that morning. Rick did not particularly like working inside, mainly because he did not like to be nice to the customers. Even being a "gopher" in the garage was better than that. But today he did not mind so much, one of the many things that seemed different about him this day. "Good morning," he said to George. "Twelve-fifty in gas and sixty-four cents for coffee . . . that'll be $13.14."

Now when Rick said, "$13.14," yet another strange thing happened. It was as if, for a moment, the whole universe collapsed in on itself and came into focus on that number—like it was the most profound utterance

The Life of Your Time

ever spoken—and something beyond the realm of space and time passed between Rick and George. George fumbled around in his billfold and finally managed to pull out $14.

Rick meant to say, "Eighty-six cents is your change," but when he opened his mouth, it seemed to come out, "There is a second chance."

"Ahem. . . well," stammered George, feeling as if his knees might buckle at any moment. "That's good to know. I'll keep it in mind."

George stepped unsteadily back away from the counter, nearly bumping into the next customer in line on his way out the door. He took off down the highway with his gas flapper open, which is the automotive equivalent of having one's fly unzipped.

Blind Chance: Ha! Look at those fools!
Chaos: But Lord Chance, you cannot look at them because you are blind.
Blind Chance: I was using a figure of speech.
Chaos: Oh, sorry.
Blind Chance: What I was going to say was how deliciously pathetic it is when the humans grope about to find ultimate meaning in their lives.
Chaos: You do seem happy in your work, sire.
Blind Chance: Work? My dear Chaos, I have elevated it to an art! Give them a coincidence or two and they think they see "the hand of God" or some such nonsense. Then hit them with a loathsome disease or a good natural disaster and watch them try to sort it all out. What fun!
Chaos: Begging my master's pardon, but aren't you supposed to dish it out more even-handedly? You sometimes seem to violate your own laws of randomness.

Blind Chance: Oh, everyone gets some, but if there wasn't a little lumpiness in the distribution of good and bad circumstances, people would get suspicious. So if I tweak it a little here and there to indulge my own fancy, who is going to fault me?

Chaos: What about that fellow Job? That seemed more than a tweak.

Blind Chance: I just never liked that guy.

Chaos: He was disgustingly good, wasn't he? But you let Lady Luck frown on him a bit, I'll say.

Blind Chance: Oh, but I couldn't have done it right without you. The boils were such a nice touch.

Chaos: Thank you, sire. I do have my moments.

Blind Chance: That reminds me, any luck locating 1314?

Chaos: Not yet, sire. I've got my best people on it—Destruction, Disintegration and Decomposition. He just manages to stay one step ahead of us. But rest assured, we'll find him.

Blind Chance: Rumor has it he is carousing with Free Will. We can't have that now, can we?

Chaos: We'll redouble our efforts, sire.

Blind Chance: See to it that you do, before this thing gets completely out of hand.

"Terry," said Velma the receptionist, poking her head into his office. "Mr. Froerking would like to see you."

"Okay. Thanks, Velma," said Terry. "Tell him I'll be there in a few minutes."

"I think he meant now," Velma said. "He seemed very upset about something."

Having worked for him many years, Velma knew Mr. Froerking and his moods as well as anyone. Terry scrambled to his feet and headed down the long corridor to Mr. Froerking's well-appointed office.

The Life of Your Time

"Bob," said Terry, "you wanted to see me?"

"That's Mr. Froerking to you!" he snapped. "Though after today it's not going to matter anyway. Don't bother to sit down. This won't take long."

Until she leaned forward, Terry had not noticed Kate sitting in one of the two high-backed leather chairs that faced Mr. Froerking's desk.

"Kate, what are you doing here?" asked Terry. "What's this all about?"

"Spare me your innocent act, Terry McKinzie," said Kate. "I know all about you and Marla!"

"But-but, there's nothing to know," Terry stammered. "Nothing happened!"

"Be quiet!" thundered Froerking. "Don't make it worse than it already is by denying it. We've got witnesses. It's all over town, for crying out loud." It was evident now how Froerking got the nickname Railroad. He was roaring like a locomotive and Terry could have sworn he saw steam coming out of his ears.

"To think I trusted you," continued Froerking. "Groomed you for the big time. And this is how you repay me—having an affair with one of your employees. I'll be lucky if we don't get sued for harassment over this. You, a married man. You had one of the all-time great women for a wife. It was bad enough you treated her like yesterday's leftovers, but to throw your marriage away over a tart like Marla . . . Well, that's just about as stupid as you can get. It grieves me to think how your parents are going to feel. It's going to absolutely kill them! A man who cheats on his wife is a man who will stop at nothing. I won't have a person like that working for me. You're fired. Did you hear that? Fired! As of right now. And furthermore, I'm going to let all my friends in the industry know just what kind of a man you are. You'll never get another decent job in radio. I guarantee it. Now, get out of my sight."

"Kate," said Terry, pleading. "You've got to believe me—"

"Tell it to someone who cares," said Kate. "I put your clothes and your golf clubs in your car, so there's no reason for you to ever set foot in my house again. In fact, I hope I never see your face again as long as I live!"

"Kate . . . Kate!" he called, reaching out for her. But she receded from his grasp.

"Terry?" said Kate, shaking him gently awake. "I'm right here. Are you okay? You were having a bad dream."

Terry opened his eyes and looked up to see Kate sitting next to him on the edge of the bed. He started to sit up, but pain shot from his chin to his neck and radiated out to his whole body. He laid his head back down on his pillow and fought the nausea that was washing over him. Kate dabbed a cool washcloth on his forehead. That helped.

"Bob called while you were asleep," said Kate gently. "Marla told him about the accident and he was concerned about you. He said to take a couple of days off—however long you want—and to let him know if you need anything. He said you've been working too hard anyway and some time away would do you some good. How do you feel?"

"I feel awful," moaned Terry, "just awful."

"I'm sure you do. That was a nasty fall," said Kate, but she did not know that was not all he meant. "Don't worry. I'll take good care of my baby."

Chapter 8

New Whirled Order

Percival slept late on Saturday morning, but that did not make him feel well rested. He shuffled sleepily down the hall, pausing briefly in the bathroom, on his way to the living room where cartoons beckoned. He was not a television junkie, but everyone knows that watching cartoons on Saturday mornings is mandatory for children. Unfortunately, sleeping late had caused him to miss Bugs Bunny, which is the only one he considered really worth watching. He surfed the channels for awhile but could not find anything that held his interest, so he gave up and went into the kitchen.

Percival's mother was sitting at the kitchen table in fuzzy slippers and a terrycloth bathrobe covering her long flannel nightgown. She was already on her second cup of coffee. Funny thing was, she didn't even like coffee and had to doctor it heavily so that she could even stomach it. But coffee helped her get going in the morning, which was becoming more and more difficult to do. She knew she should have cooked Percival some breakfast, but excused herself on account of George going in to work. She watched as he poured himself a bowl of Rice Crispies. "Wasn't it just yesterday I brought him home from the hospital?" she thought. "He's growing up so fast."

The cereal was consumed in near silence. That is to say no words were exchanged, although there could never be total silence when Rice Crispies are being eaten—at least until they get soggy.

Ann kept thinking she should say something. Percival seemed so pensive lately. But then she thought perhaps she was projecting her own mood onto him, so she said nothing. She sipped at her coffee and fought back the feeling that something very important had gotten away from her.

* * * * *

George did not go straight home. He needed time to think. Somehow, the interstate did not seem like the right place to sort out the thoughts that were swirling around in his head, so he took the next exit and headed west toward no place in particular.

The coffee was stronger than usual today. Must be the new kid, George thought. What was that he said about a second chance? He must have misheard him. Or maybe he was on drugs or something. He looked the type. Except for his eyes. He seemed earnest. Okay, maybe he was not on drugs. It was not nice to stereotype people.

But why would he think George needed a second chance? He had done all right. He had been at the same company for twenty-eight years. So he was not a vice president, so what. He had been a valuable employee. The Baileys always liked him. They knew him by name. They said he helped them build the company. And he did. He had been a team player. A guy they could depend on.

And what about Ann and Percival? He had been a good husband and father—better than most. He did not spend all his time playing golf. Quality family time—that was the key. And a good provider. Steady. They had a nice place to live. Always plenty to eat. The bills always got paid. Maybe they did not have a lot of luxuries on his salary, but Ann had simple tastes. She did not mind, did she? She never complained. Come to think of it, they had not talked much at all lately. Oh, there was small talk. Always pleasant. They rarely argued. But not much beyond that. After fifteen years, you start running out of things to say. Or was it sixteen? George could never remember for sure.

Was it just his imagination, or had she seemed withdrawn lately? Hard to tell for sure with women, he thought. Feelings running all over the place. It was a mystery to him. Maybe he would make more of an effort to talk to her. Yes. Draw her out. Be sensitive. He was a good husband.

And look at Percival. What more could you ask for in a child? Good grades. Good manners. Not a smart aleck like most of the kids today. He had done all right in the father department, too. What was it Percival was trying to ask him the other day? Oh, well. He would worry about that later. He had not done that bad a job in life. He had not messed up his first chance. What did he need with a second?

*****

What was left of the morning passed slowly for Percival. He went into his room and played with his Legos for awhile, but could not think of anything

The Life of Your Time

inspiring to build. He tried to pick up where he left off on *Alice in Wonderland,* but decided he was not in the mood to read either. He went outside and wandered restlessly around the yard. If he would have had a dog, he would have petted it. Finally, he sat down on the old tractor tire that had been converted into a makeshift sandbox.

"I'm really getting too big for sandboxes," he thought as he scratched around in it with the end of a stick. "Probably too big for a lot of things."

He had been trying his best to avoid thinking about things that happen which make a person wonder. After all, it was probably just—what did Mrs. Thomas call it?—oh yes, a coincidence.

Percival rolled the word around in his mind several times, pronouncing it different ways and emphasizing different syllables. He decided that it must have come from the root word "coin," so it likely had something to do with money. And that led him to the thought that just about everything had to do with money. Karen was probably right. Life was about getting ahead. Survival of the fittest. No point in feeling bad about cutting in line. After all, it had been his turn. Just because he didn't know it, well, what difference did it make? He had given up his turn lots of times. They owed it to him. He might just do it again on Monday. And every day. That would show them. This nice guy stuff was for losers!

"I'm one of the smartest kids in class," Percival said to himself. "I could go a long way in life. Karen said so and she always knows what she is talking about. I'm going to make something of myself. Yes. And if anyone gets in my way, they better look out. And then I'll marry Karen. Well, maybe not. But she will know that I'm not somebody to be trifled with. Killer instinct and all that."

New Whirled Order

If Mr. Wimbley could have witnessed this scene, he would have been proud. The more Percival psyched himself up, the more he liked himself. He began to fancy himself a famous writer, traveling all over the world writing important things. He would wear sunglasses—even indoors. And when he got his driver's license, he would drive a very expensive car. And people would think he was a very important person because he wrote very important things. And then he would not have to crowd in line any more. People would gladly give up their places for him and maybe even carry him on their shoulders to the front of the line. And on and on it went, until he felt devilishly good about himself.

The sound of a heart hardening, if it could be heard, is a sickening sound—so sickening, in fact, that if it *were* audible, people might take more care to avoid it. While there is no direct analogy in time and space, it might be compared with the sound of an automobile running over a turtle. Very slowly.

* * * * *

From her upstairs bedroom window, Ann watched Percival scratching around in the sandbox. He was hard to read, she thought. Like his father, he was a true Weckbaugh. But she sensed that something was troubling him. She longed to go to him and comfort him and tell him everything was going to be all right. But, not being convinced of this herself, she did not know if she could convince him. Perhaps that would be a disservice anyway. Maybe it is better to find out young. No point in getting his hopes up. The disappointment would just be that much greater.

She reached for a picture frame from her dresser—a photograph of Percival when he was a toddler.

"Where does the time go?" she thought as she caressed the picture. She studied it for signs of herself—eyes, nose, mouth. But she concluded, as she had many times in the past, that Percival was pretty thoroughly a Weckbaugh. Not that this was a bad thing. After all, she was quite fond of Weckbaughs in general and George and Percival in particular. It was just that she felt as though something were missing in her—something she once had but was now lost. Not only did she not have any idea where she might have misplaced it, she was not exactly sure what it was. She looked at the picture another long moment, hoping she might get a clue from the photo. She found none.

As she replaced the picture on the dresser shelf, she caught her own reflection in the mirror. The October sun was low enough in the sky to shine directly into the bedroom at midday and the bright light accentuated the lines on her face. Thirty-eight, she thought. Definitely on the high side of thirty-something. Thirty-seven could still be generously construed as mid-thirties, but thirty-eight, she had to conclude, was unquestionably upper thirties. Forty was in plain view. She looked old, she thought. She used to be pretty, but now she just looked old. She started to check her high school graduation picture to confirm that she had, in fact, been pretty once, but stopped. It was too painful to be reminded that graphically of how far she had fallen. Better the abstract—the idea that she had once been pretty—than the reality. And talented. Worlds of potential. Where had it all gone?

From somewhere in the back of her mind came the faint echo of a song. Somehow, she knew it was important, but she could not remember what it was. Like so many other things in her life, it had slipped away from her.

New Whirled Order

In her mind, Ann drifted back in time to an opportunity she once had and the boy who offered it to her. A chance to go on the road and live in the limelight. Maybe even stardom.

She did not exactly regret her decision. After all, she loved George very much and could not have asked for a gentler partner to spend her life with. And Percival was a model child. She had been content to be a homemaker. She had made the right decision. But the spectre of what might have been haunted her. And what was that song she was trying to remember?

Ann turned away—away from the dresser, away from the reminder of what could have been and walked out of the bedroom and down the stairs. The big Victorian house that had once charmed her so seemed oppressive these days. "I should get out more," she thought. But even as the thought crossed her mind she knew she would not. Out there were disappointed looks and questioning eyes she did not want to look into. She knew what they were thinking: *Why did she throw away such a promising career? Why did she just waste her talent?*

Ann put on the sweater that hung on a peg in the hallway. The old house was drafty, she thought. Never properly weatherized. Cold in the winter, hot in the summer and seldom just right. The utilities were always too high. Maybe they should just move. It would be closer for George to work. And further from a small town turned suburb that was feeling more and more like a prison camp.

She went to the piano. Although her greatest gift was singing, she had at one time been a superior pianist as well. She tried to think how long it had been since she sat down and played it. Without the discipline of practice, her skills deteriorated. And then it became frustrating to struggle with pieces she had once played well. And that frustration only discouraged her from playing all the more until she finally gave it up altogether. The Weckbaugh boys were not musically inclined and she had long since despaired of giving lessons to Percival. Try as he might, he just never quite seemed to get the hang of it. She knew he was only doing it for her benefit anyway, so she stopped. Now the piano was just a useless piece of furniture.

Ann opened the lid of the bench and began leafing through the sheet music and lesson books searching for the piece that she could not quite remember. Tears welled up in her eyes when she ran across *Sailboats*, her first contest piece. She must have been what—five or six? That had been a happier time—full of wonder and possibilities and hope. Not like now. She recalled a fragment of the song she was trying to remember. There was a sea in it as well. But this one was not inhabited by sailboats. No, this was a sea of sorrows breaking over her like huge ocean swells.

She went to the closet and began hauling out old boxes of sheet music and song books that had been packed away for years. Frantically, she searched for the missing song. She wished her mother was alive. She would remember. She always knew the right thing to say. The sting of her loss was still fresh in her memory.

That was how Percival found her—sitting cross-legged on the floor with boxes and music strewn all over the room.

"Mom?" asked Percival. "Are you okay?"

She did not want to lie, so she said nothing. Percival carefully picked his way through the piles of paper to where she was sitting. He could tell she had been crying. He knew the signs well by now. The eyes always gave her away.

"I—I was looking for something," she finally managed to say. "Something I misplaced."

"I'll help you look for it," Percival offered.

She shook her head and said, "It doesn't matter now. It really wasn't important."

"It's okay, Mom," he said as he patted her head. "Really, it's okay." And then he helped her re-pack the boxes.

* * * * *

The bright October sun felt good on George's face. The combination of the sunshine and stiff coffee had warmed him up, so he cracked the window. Ah, the fresh country air, he thought. They should really get out more. The world really was not such a bad place. And if there was more to it than meets the eye, so much the better, right? He was not against religion. He just had not given it much thought. There probably was something more. That was not a bad thing. Of course not. But what was it doing in his computer?

The answer to this question did not readily present itself and George did not have much experience along these lines from which to draw. Yet there it was intruding into his life. It was a neat and tidy life and he liked it that way. This was messy.

"But if there is something more, that would be important," he thought. "Maybe the most important thing of all." This alarmed him. If there was something more, how could he have missed it for fifty-two years? That would have meant something. It would have made a difference in his life. "And what does it want with me?" he wondered. "Who am I that I would even be on his mind at all? Is he trying to say something to me? And what was it about the kid at the gas station?"

The Life of Your Time

George braked hard and pulled onto a dirt road that led to who-knows-where out in the middle of nowhere. He got out and leaned on the side of his car. Looking out over the subtle beauty of the Flint Hills with its prairie grass stretched thinly and at times unevenly over the rocky rolling hills, George realized that he had no idea where he was.

Some people have the ability to hold multiple ideas in their minds simultaneously. They often make great leaders, whether chief executive officers or quarterbacks. They see the panorama of options in a given situation and have the ability to quickly decide on the optimal path. It is also true that their breadth of understanding must frequently come at the expense of depth of understanding. And if a leader does not explore every option to its ultimate degree, most people would not fault them for that—unless, of course, it turns out to be an unpopular decision and then there is always lots of second guessing.

George was not that type of thinker; rather the opposite. When he fixed his mind on a subject, he tended to burrow way down, which is one of the primary reasons he was good at what he did. But this singlemindedness of focus also involved a tradeoff, and what he traded was attention to anything else. He had a remarkable ability to tune everything else out except what he was focusing on, which was why Ann checked his clothing carefully before he left each morning to prevent embarrassing color combinations or glaring omissions. Both kinds of thinkers are needed in the world, although at present there seems to be an overabundance of people who do not seem to do much thinking at all.

Now it was this type of tunnel vision that had led George to the present predicament in more ways than one. He began to experience a feeling not only of lost-

New Whirled Order

ness in the realization that the universe was much different than he had perceived it, but also of dread at the implications of having missed something so profound.

Suddenly, he missed Ann and Percival very much and with that came a feeling that somehow he had let them down. He got back in his car and headed back in the direction from which he had come, searching for a landmark so he could find his way home.

About three miles back up the road he saw a rancher feeding his calves. So urgent was George's sense that he needed to get home right away, that he stopped and asked for directions which, as everyone knows, is abhorrent to all men.

* * * * *

By the time George got home, everything was back in order in the Weckbaugh home. Ann sat with Percival in the kitchen as he ate his afternoon snack. George sat down next to Percival and looked him straight in the eye. In a very serious tone, he said, "I think it does mean something."

Percival nodded understandingly. Ann, however, was perplexed. "What are you two talking about?"

So Percival told her about the clock incident and then George told both of them about the strange things that happened to him. When both had finished speaking, there was a long moment of silence that was finally broken by George's startling announcement: "Tomorrow, we are all going to church."

Blind Chance: These humans really are a sorry lot. So
    few of them have had the guts to face reality.
    Except maybe the existentialists. Now those were
    real men. You didn't hear any drivel about ulti-

The Life of Your Time

mate meaning coming from their lips. Makes me a little nostalgic just thinking about it. Whatever happened to all the good existentialists?

Chaos: I think most of them either ended up in mental institutions or took their own lives, sire.

Blind Chance: Pity. But we're having a lot more fun without them, eh Chaos? Think how boring it would be for us if everyone gave up the whole "meaning of life" delusion.

Chaos (weakly): If you say so, sir.

Blind Chance: You don't sound convinced.

Chaos: I think I'm just a little run down today.

Blind Chance: That's bad?

Chaos: All this roaming around here and there spreading disorder all the time wears a person out. I just can't seem to get organized . . .

Blind Chance: Now there's one of the all-time brilliant statements! You're *Chaos,* you idiot! You're *supposed* to be disorganized!

Chaos: I'm well aware of that. I only meant that it's a monumental task. And Order has me at a distinct disadvantage.

Blind Chance: How many times must I command you not to use that name in my presence! There is no such thing as order—just a lack of disorder. It's only an illusion. All of it is just one big series of accidents. A random, purposeless, sequence of events. And none of it means anything!

Chaos: All I know is when you spend all your time unraveling the universe, it makes you wonder how it all got raveled to begin with.

Blind Chance: I worry about you sometimes.

* * * * *

"Hey, Rick," said Doug when Rick came to the phone.

"Hey, yourself," said Rick. There was an awkward moment of silence during which Doug momentarily wondered if he had made a mistake by calling.

Rick, though, was simply stunned by the voice on the other end. Their last conversation, as nearly as he could remember it, had not gone well and he had said some things he now regretted. But with the cat-like quality of (nearly) always landing on his feet, Rick tried to recover, "I can't believe it's you. I figured you'd be out celebrating the big win."

"You heard?" asked Doug.

"I listened to the game on the radio at work."

"Really? The guys did all right today."

"What are you talking about 'all right,'" said Rick. "You played great. The announcer said you were just running over your man. And two receptions. Where'd you get those hands?"

"I got a hand transplant," said Doug. "Haven't you heard? They're doing some amazing things these days."

"Sounds like a miracle," said Rick.

"That's for sure," said Doug. "So, anyway, how are you doing, man?"

There was a long pause because Rick was unsure how to respond. "I don't know, Doug," he said, suddenly serious. "Things have been kind of rough lately."

This came as no revelation to Doug, because he had known all along that Rick was headed for trouble. However, he was surprised that Rick would admit it since he was the kind of person who always gave off the impression that he had it together, regardless of the circumstances. "Sorry to hear that," was all Doug could think of to say.

The Life of Your Time

"Hey, you don't need to be sorry," said Rick. "It's nobody's fault but my own. You tried to tell me, but I wouldn't listen. You know I hate it when you're right."

"I remember," said Doug.

"But I'm gonna get it together. Seriously. I even got my hair cut this afternoon after work."

"That is serious."

"Yeah, the old man about had a stroke. Anyway, I'm glad you called. I was thinking about old times today." Rick paused and then said, "Maybe we could get together sometime."

"How about tomorrow," said Doug, seizing the opportunity. "I've got some free time after church."

To this, Rick replied, "Cool," which, for the slang-impaired, should be translated, "Really? That would be great. I look forward to seeing you then."

As he hung up the phone, Rick mused on the timing of this call. It added to the exhilarating sensation of life he was experiencing today—a sense that only someone who had had a near brush with the alternative could fully appreciate.

* * * * *

"Mr. Froerking?" Terry said when the old gentleman answered the phone.

"Is that you, Terry?" Mr. Froerking said, wondering briefly why Terry did not call him Bob. "How are you feeling this afternoon? Heard you had a nasty fall."

"I feel pretty rough right now, but I'll survive," said Terry. "Listen, I'm sorry to bother you at home on a Saturday, but I wanted to take you up on your offer to help. It's not for me, actually. It's for Kate. You know she's into art and I heard that the Monet exhibit is opening at the Nelson next week and I was wondering . . . ."

"If I would pull some strings and get you tickets to the VIP reception?"

"Well, yes," said Terry. "You do have connections."

"Are you saying you can't afford that sort of thing on your salary?" Froerking prodded.

"My boss has a reputation for being tighter than bark on a tree," said Terry, picking up on Froerking's lead. He could tell by the tone in his voice that the man would do anything he asked. "Besides, I heard it was sold out anyway, so I couldn't get tickets now even if I could afford it."

"I'll see what I can do," said Froerking. "For her sake, mind you, not yours."

"Understood," said Terry, wondering why men have to talk in code language when they want to be nice to each other.

"After all, she is one of the all-time great women," said Froerking. "You're lucky to have her."

"That's for sure," said Terry, wincing at a fresh twinge of pain in his chin. As he hung up the phone, he repeated to himself, "That is for sure."

Chapter 9

Call of the Mild

Percival had attended Sunday School a time or two with friends, but not recently. This Sunday, though, seemed different. He felt a sense of urgency and expectancy about it that he had not experienced before.

The sixth-grade class was taught by Col. Adrian Martin. This was not primarily because no one else wanted to teach a class of unruly sixth-graders, nor was it because Colonel Martin had demonstrated throughout his life that he had the mettle to handle the toughest assignments. The main reason was because he wanted to make a difference in the lives of these young people.

The classroom resided in the back corner of the church basement and smelled faintly musty as basements often do. Books lined the far wall and other resource material was stacked neatly on shelves. On an easel in the corner, flannel figures were arranged with the precision of a military campaign map. Today's pictures depicted Daniel in the Lion's Den.

The Life of Your Time

Col. Martin related the facts about Daniel's experience in mission briefing style. That is not to say, however, that his presentation was in any way dry or boring. On the contrary, the Colonel was a gifted storyteller and the students listened in rapt attention, punctuated only by occasional "oohs" and "ahs" at the appropriate points.

Percival, though, had trouble concentrating on the details of the story. His mind was preoccupied with a dilemma of cosmic proportions: a longing to know an answer to a question he could not formulate (the formulation of such question being akin to the aforementioned difficulty of trying to smell music).

The previous day, he had been ready to abandon his seeking—to try to avoid altogether thinking thoughts that make a person wonder. After all, seeking answers to unformulated questions was a difficult enough endeavor. But if there was no answer to find, if there was no ultimate purpose behind the universe, if all of life was essentially meaningless, then the act of seeking was itself a vain pursuit.

Although he could not yet express his feelings in words or even thoughts, he had begun to suspect that such a quest might be a waste of time. Already, the quest had gotten him in trouble at school. He had spent hours now worrying about it and hours can seem like years to young boys. Perhaps it would be better to expunge such notions from his mind. Maybe he should concentrate instead on falling in step with the world with which he felt so out of step. Possibly even try to get ahead. After all, it was a jungle out there and only the fittest survived. And in a dog-eat-dog universe, survival was the only logical purpose of existence. If he had just given up, most people would not have faulted him. Then, again, most people had not even made it that far.

But just when his quest seemed doomed, his father's strange experiences had inexplicably renewed his hope. Perhaps he was not alone, then, in feeling that there might be more to the world than meets the eye. Perhaps forces he did not understand were at work around him. Perhaps—though he was not sure that he should even hope this hope—he might by some means come to understand something of these forces he did not understand.

Yet herein lay another problem to complicate an already difficult situation: Percival realized that he needed help, because he had no idea where to begin looking for knowledge pertaining to these possibly existing forces he did not understand. The Clock Incident had just happened. He was not looking for something to happen nor even aware that he should be watching for something. But now that he was searching, he felt he could definitely use some guidance. He had lived nearly twelve years before he found this first clue and he did not think he could wait twelve more for the next. If only someone could point him in the right direction.

But finding someone who could be trusted in a world where trustworthiness was in woefully short supply was a daunting task in itself. Normally, his father was the person he turned to for answers. But his father seemed to be just as baffled by it all as he was.

Furthermore, Percival, as has been noted, was not a person inclined to share his inmost thoughts and feelings; and recent events, if anything, had caused him to be even more circumspect than usual. Still, though, he had a yearning in his heart to know something—even if he did not know what that something was—and that yearning outweighed his reticence. In a way, the vagueness of his yearning served to heighten his senses. Every experience now seemed as if it might be loaded with meaning. He was afraid he might miss some important clue, so his mind was fully alert. Every person he encountered was a potential source of illumination and here, across the table from him, was the leading candidate for the moment. Instead of fully listening to Col. Martin's words, Percival listened to the man, sizing him up to determine if he was a person who could be trusted.

"The Colonel," as he was respectfully known, was a retired Air Force navigator, held in high regard by all the locals and most especially the young boys. He had a closely-cropped military haircut that now showed more silver than black, accenting his angular features. He was taller than average, but not enormous, so perhaps it was the way he carried himself that made him seem larger than he was. Or perhaps it was the authority and dignity of his manner. Perhaps most important of all, it may have been an intangible quality of *being* that manifested itself in everything he did.

Not even his limp could detract from his presence—a limp caused by an injury sustained upon crash landing after being shot down over the jungles of Vietnam; a limp that probably would have been considerably less noticeable had he received proper medical care instead of neglect in a POW camp; a limp that had been highly decorated by his government although it had not been especially appreciated by the general public at the time; and a limp that even today caused him varying degrees of pain. But somehow the limp seemed to add to, rather than detract from, who he was.

"Here is a man who has stared into the face of Death," thought Percival by the time class ended.

Call of the Mild

"And he lived to tell about it. Maybe he would understand."

*****

George was nervous, which was unusual for him. He was not a nervous person, but church was unfamiliar territory. He had gotten married in a church and been to a few funerals. Outside of that, he had never had much to do with them. He had no idea what he expected to happen and was not sure why he was even there. All he had was a vague sense that God might be trying to tell him something and he reasoned that church was a logical place to try to sort it out.

The regular adult Sunday School classes had been preempted for a presentation by missionaries to Chile whom the church supported. George found the program, complete with slides, to be quite interesting. Although he had never done much traveling himself, he enjoyed hearing about other cultures. The missionaries had experienced many adventures and even a few close brushes with danger. The presentation was, in fact, so entertaining that George began to think that church might not be such a bad sort of place after all. He even began to imagine that he might like to travel to exotic places and have adventures of his own, though he had only the vaguest notion of why the missionaries had gone there in the first place.

Now, though, sitting there in a pew waiting for the worship service to begin, he was not so sure this was for him after all. You see, thinking about being in other places is relatively easy, even enjoyable. But thinking about *being* in general is another matter entirely. The former, which one might call material thinking (that is, thinking about people, places and things), allows for a certain amount of detachment.

The Life of Your Time

That is to say that one's mind can be stimulated, pleasantly or unpleasantly, without a great deal of personal investment. In this sense, it is rather like watching television. You can love or hate the characters and laugh or cry at what happens to them. But when the show is over, you can turn off the television and go on about your business. Unless, of course, you get addicted to the programs and they begin to make demands on your life by crowding out other, perhaps more fruitful, pursuits. Yet, in this sense, the analogy holds up well in that material thinking tends to crowd out deep thinking just like watching television crowds out real living.

Not so with thinking about being or, for want of a better term, spiritual thinking (you cannot properly call it immaterial thinking as that includes other kinds of abstractions not under consideration here). Spiritual thoughts, by their very nature, make demands upon their thinker. They lie very close to the core of our being, which is their principle concern, and the very act of thinking them effects change. Therefore, at their best, they can be unsettling. At their worst, they can bring about fear or even despair.

Thus, the fact that George, who had never given much thought to spiritual matters, was uncomfortable should come as no surprise. That is not to say, though, that his stoic countenance betrayed any such feeling. But if you looked closely at his left foot, which was crossed over his right knee, you would notice that it was rotating slowly clockwise—a sure sign he was nervous. After awhile, he switched legs and began slowly rotating his right foot counter-clockwise which, for George, indicated that he was nearly frantic.

* * * * *

Call of the Mild

Two rows in front of the Weckbaughs, Doug Martin, nearly a full head taller than anyone else around him, sat proudly between his parents and his grandparents. But although his body sat still, his heart did not. In a manner of speaking, it was soaring somewhere in the stratosphere. He had much for which to be thankful—his blossoming football career, his budding relationship with Nancy, and the seeds of hope he had detected in Rick. You might even say he felt blessed.

Doug caught a glimpse of the Colonel out of the corner of his eye and noted the expression on his rugged face—the one that seemed to look beyond. Doug wondered, as he had many times before, what it was that he saw. It puzzled him that, whether times were good or bad, happy or sad, the look never changed except in intensity.

As Doug pondered this mystery, it suddenly occurred to him that perhaps the enigma of the unchanging expression was its own answer. It did not change with circumstances because it did not depend upon circumstances.

Doug reflected on his own life and considered whether, if all the good things in his life went bad tomorrow, he would bear up as well. It was an uncomfortable question or, more precisely, a question that had uncomfortable answers. Those uncomfortable answers troubled him, but it was not necessarily a bad sort of trouble because it triggered within him a desire to change. "Someday," Doug thought wishfully, "maybe I'll have that look, too."

* * * * *

Though Doug did not yet know her, Nancy's sister Kate and her husband Terry were sitting right across the aisle from him. They were casual and rather sporadic attendees, but Terry was under a conviction he could not explain that he needed to be there that day. Even though he still felt groggy, he dragged himself out of bed and went, stitches and all. As a matter of fact, he was, at the moment, feeling rather self-satisfied that he had made such an heroic effort to be there.

Kate and Terry sat next to the Froerkings. When Mr. Froerking winked at him, Terry smiled smugly to himself. That meant the Monet opening tickets were his. He could not wait to tell Kate—she would be thrilled. And his guilty conscience would be assuaged.

As one who in public places had an inclination toward wanting to see and be seen, Terry nonchalantly scanned the sanctuary and nodded at several people he recognized. Then, his eyes met Percival's and they locked on each other.

Terry knew he had seen the kid somewhere before, but could not quite place him. Percival, noting Terry's quizzical expression, slowly, gravely raised his left arm—the one on which he wore his watch—for the Clock Man to see. Terry quickly looked down at his own wrist. He had never gotten around to buying a new battery for his. And while that may have seemed a trivial matter to most, the thought suddenly alarmed him.

When Terry realized where he had seen Percival before, the smug smile vanished from his face. Then, his skin began to tingle—the sort of feeling one might expect right before being struck by lightning.

In an overwhelming flash of insight that was every bit as powerful as a thunderbolt, Terry transcended the ordinary understanding of time and saw it for the first moment in his life from the cosmic point of view. When comprehended from the vantage point of eternity, temporal distinctions marked by clocks and calendars dissolve into insignificance. Time, in this cosmic sense, is always the same. The unbending reality of it shook Terry down to the very depths of his being as he realized: *It is later than you think.*

* * * * *

Just as the prelude began, Rick Callahan, short-haired and contrite, managed to successfully dodge the greeters and slipped into the church unnoticed. He felt quite ill-at-ease. In his perception, this was a place for the upstanding citizens of Central City—not down-and-outers like him. He thought if they knew half the things he had done, they probably would have posted an armed guard at the door to keep him out. The urge to turn around and escape swelled within him. But he had made some promises and, for a change, he intended to keep them.

Rick's general impression of church-going people was that, for the most part, they were a bunch of holier-than-thou hypocrites who were always looking down their noses at everybody else. The idea of people pretending to be something they were not turned his stomach. But just as this thought was crossing his mind, he noticed a sign on the wall that he guessed must have been the church's slogan: "A Place to Belong."

It suddenly occurred to Rick that he himself might not be so far removed from hypocrisy as he had imagined. Had he not always pretended to have his life together even when he did not? Had he not shunned his old friends to impress his cool new ones? ("Cool," being an extremely useful word for Rick with a wide range of meanings, in this sense indicated higher class, popular and in vogue.) And, had he not at that

The Life of Your Time

very moment been "looking down his nose" with contempt at the very people whom he perceived were "looking down their noses" at him?

"Maybe I do belong," thought Rick, "right here in the Hypocrite Club." He found a relatively deserted section near the back corner of the sanctuary, sat down and stared at the floor.

* * * * *

Ann Weckbaugh had been shocked by George's decision to come that morning. It was so atypical of him, she thought. George rarely did anything impulsively. He did not always talk about what he was thinking of doing, which could give a false impression of spontaneity when he suddenly acted on his thoughts. But Ann knew better—that George seldom did anything large or small without careful consideration. So when he suggested something as madcap as attending church, it caught her totally unprepared. As far as she had known, this had been the furthest thing from his mind.

The more Ann had reflected upon it, though, the better she had felt about it. Growing up, she had attended church regularly. Her parents rarely missed and the weekly ritual was as regular as clockwork in their lives. Yet, as the years went by, she attended less and less frequently. It was not a conscious decision. Rather, she was like a swimmer who ceases all efforts against the outgoing tide and gradually drifts away.

Many heads had turned as she entered the sanctuary, but Ann ignored them. Her avoidance of eye contact was well practiced. Now, waiting for the service to begin, she experienced a sense of anticipation. It had been a long time, she thought—too long.

Call of the Mild

When the instrumentalists struck the opening chords of the first song, an incredible wave of emotion swept over her. Suddenly, she remembered the words to the song she had forgotten and did not even need to open her hymnal as she sang:

When peace like a river attendeth my way,
When sorrows like sea billows roll;
Whatever my lot, Thou hast taught me to say,
"It is well, it is well with my soul."

* * * * *

Percival tried to concentrate during the service, but his mind kept wandering. He had been thinking about Col. Martin, who was sitting a few rows in front of him, when the Clock Man distracted him. At least it looked like the Clock Man, except for the bandage.

What had happened to the Clock Man, Percival could only speculate. "Maybe he got struck with a meteor in the face," he thought. "After all, the universe is a dangerous place with the conspiracy and all." Percival began to entertain the idea of asking the Clock Man after church if he had any insights about their strange shared experience and whether he thought it held any meaning relative to the mysteries of the universe and the meaning of existence.

He glanced in the Clock Man's direction again. "No, better leave him alone," thought Percival. "He looks really scared or something. Better stick with the Colonel. He's different. I don't know how, but he's different. The Colonel knows something. You can tell by the look in his eyes. He knows something."

* * * * *

The Life of Your Time

George sat unmoved during the service, trying to suppress feelings of disappointment as his rotating foot gradually ground to a halt. The sermon was on the Good Samaritan and, lest there be any confusion on this point, let it be known that the minister did the text justice. Love your neighbor—that was good, thought George. Help the needy—a fine thing to do.

But frankly, while it was a good message, it was exactly the sort of sermon he would have expected. Although he did not have much personal experience upon which to draw, he had some preconceived notions of churches and ministers that were not entirely inaccurate—namely, that their stock in trade was this very type of morality and good-deed doing. Of course, he had nothing against morality and good-deed doing. After all, he considered himself the kind of person of whom these traits could be said to apply. No serious vices. No skeletons hidden in the closet. "I've been a decent man," he thought. "I support the United Way. And didn't I just give money to the boy down the street who was collecting for Jerry's kids?"

And herein lay the primary reason George had never perceived much need to attend church. He was a pretty good person without it. Better than most, now that he thought about it. Therefore, while a healthy dose of morality teaching was what he expected from church, it was not exactly the experience for which he might have hoped. Not that he was necessarily looking for miracles or blinding flashes of light. As he reflected on it, he did not have any clear or conscious idea what he expected.

Secretly, though, while he may have resisted admitting it to himself, perhaps he had hoped not for the expected, but for the unexpected. Maybe even an answer. He left without any.

Call of the Mild

* * * * *

After the service, Rick slipped quickly out the back and loitered in the parking lot waiting for Doug. Rick had spotted him during the service, which was not a difficult feat considering that Doug towered above the rest of the crowd. Rick was still amazed at Doug's phone call yesterday seemingly out of the blue. After all, Rick had not exactly been a model friend and he had previously doubted that Doug ever wanted to see him again. But now, he realized more than ever that Doug had been the only true friend he had ever had.

George was concentrating on the traffic exiting the church parking lot, so he did not notice the young man from the gas station and, with Rick's newly shorn hair, might not have recognized him if he did. But Ann noticed him—the gaunt stranger with the dark, haunting eyes. She could not place him, yet somehow he looked familiar. As they drove away, she could not help thinking she had seen those eyes before.

When Doug came out with his family, Rick cocked his head. As soon as Doug recognized who it was, he told his family to go on and came on a dead run, arms wide and ground quaking under his steps. Momentarily, Rick thought he was going to tackle him, but he just grabbed him instead and lifted him off his feet.

"Whoa, Popeye!" said Rick. "You've been eatin' too much spinach."

"Coach has had us pumping some major iron," said Doug. "I had to buy new shirts. The old ones wouldn't fit anymore."

There was an awkward moment of silence and Doug looked around trying to think of something to say. Finally, he said, "So, what's with the hair? I hardly recognized you."

The Life of Your Time

"Didn't I tell you? I'm joining the Marines."

"Yeah, right," said Doug. That was typical Rick, he thought. Never a straight answer.

"Seriously, though, I just . . ." Rick's voice trailed off. "I just wanted to make some changes."

Doug nodded, but did not say anything, noting that this was *not* typical Rick. Not the fun-loving Rick he had known growing up. Not the wise-cracking party animal he later became. And not even the upbeat, new-attitude Rick he had talked to yesterday.

Rick took a pack of cigarettes from the pocket of his black leather jacket and lit one, but he knew Doug well enough not to offer. He took a long drag and wondered if he could put into words what he was feeling or if he should even try. Gone was the exhilaration and near euphoria he had experienced yesterday. The bleak facts of his life had regrouped and made a fresh assault on his psyche. Once again, he felt himself being pulled down the pathway to despair.

"Do you remember the time when your Dad caught us smoking behind the garage?" asked Rick.

"Are you kidding? He tanned my hide good."

"It says right on the package, 'This product may be hazardous to your health.'"

"It sure was," said Doug. "I never had much desire to do it again."

"You know, that's the difference," Rick said gravely. "Between you and me, I mean. You learned your lessons. You listened. You didn't just keep making the same mistakes over and over. Me—it just made me want to go out and do something even worse."

He took another long draw and said, "But now . . . now that the dance is over, it's time to pay the piper. Do you know what I mean? I hate the face that stares back at me in the mirror."

Call of the Mild

Doug wanted to say something, but there was no denying the truth. He stared and stared hard at this person he thought he knew—his old friend, his intimate confidant. Rick was like a photographic negative of himself: everything he was, Rick was not. Looking into that negative image was like looking into a magical mirror—not one that reflected the way things are, but one that showed the way things might have been. And, at that moment, Doug knew, more fully than he ever had in his life, that he could not take credit for the difference.

"I've hit bottom," said Rick at last. "A black hole. It's about to swallow me up. And I don't know how to find my way out again." His voice trailed off. "I don't know if there *is* a way out."

"There is," said Doug, almost as much for his own benefit as Rick's. "We'll find it."

"After the way I've treated you, why would you want to help a loser like me?"

Doug laid his gigantic right hand on Rick's shoulder and said with fervent simplicity, "Because I'm your friend."

Chapter 10

Behind the Seen

Sunday dinner at the Weckbaugh home passed in relative silence. What each of them really wanted to say seemed awkward to discuss. Percival was so absorbed in pondering what he would do next, he could not even have told you what he ate.

After dinner, Percival executed his plan, beginning with finding Col. Martin's address in the phone book. As nowhere is too far from anywhere in a small town, he found that it was only a few blocks away from his own home. Calculating that he could get there without crossing any major thoroughfares, he asked his parents if it would be okay if he rode his bike around the neighborhood for awhile. Then he set out on the next leg of his quest.

* * * * *

George began clearing dishes from the table, but Ann shooed him away from the kitchen. She could tell he needed to think and, since she felt unusually energized, she did not need his help.

Ann hummed to herself as she cleaned. She could not quite put her finger on it, but it was as if something inside her was reawakening, something that had been dormant for a long time. She wanted to tell George and Percival that something was happening to her, but she did not know how to go about it since she was not quite sure what it was. The feeling was wonderful and fearful, gentle but overpowering, and definitely something not to be ignored. So she gave way to it and allowed herself to be swept along. Before long, with her arms in dishwater nearly up to her elbows, she was singing out loud.

As she did so, all sorts of memories danced in her mind—memories of other songs and old times. She thought of voice lessons, roles she had performed in musicals and special songs she had sung. They were thoughts she had not allowed herself to think for a long time. And while some of the memories were bittersweet, on this particular day, they seemed less bitter and more sweet. She even remembered her old band Sylvan Dream and the crazy times they had together.

Then she stopped washing and stared out the window as two thoughts suddenly connected in her mind. One memory seemed a lifetime ago. The other was as fresh as that morning when she had seen the young man under the tree in the church parking lot. And she thought, "He has his brother's eyes."

* * * * *

George retired to the living room, sat down in his easy chair and lit his pipe. It was his one vice, and only an occasional one at that. But it helped him to relax, and edgy as he felt, that was the effect he was hoping to achieve. As the sweet cherry tobacco smoke wafted upward, George found himself wondering if that was like what happened to people when they died—if their souls rose up to the sky. Or did they just dissipate like the smoke?

He did not know the answer and that frustrated him. The more he thought about it, the more important the question became. After all, forever would be a very long time. If there were even a slight chance that something beyond this world existed after death, it would be a matter of supreme importance. And if there was even the remotest possibility that what you did with your earthly life had a bearing on the one that came after, it was only prudent to give the matter your utmost attention.

"But what now?" George asked himself as he puffed thoughtfully on his pipe. The idea that God was more than just a mindless cosmic force or a divine computer programmer who just programmed the world to run and then went away was a novel one to him. But if God was more than that, if He was a God who was concerned about the details . . .

His thoughts lingered there for awhile as he struggled to complete the thought. But the task proved impossible because it is beyond human ability to ascertain by reason alone. And George, being an unusually bright person, realized the futility of it. He thought, "How could I possibly know unless—"

The "unless," of course, was that God would reveal His purposes to him. Perhaps God, George reasoned, had taken the initiative to communicate with him when He made his computer do something it was not programmed to do. Maybe God was waiting for a response from him.

What George, the eminently rational man, did next might seem irrational to most people. But at this particular point in his life, it seemed about as logical a course of action as any. He set his pipe aside, went into the study, and booted up their home computer.

The Life of Your Time

Logging onto the Internet, he wrote and launched this simple message to God: "I'm listening."

He nearly fell out of his chair when the "ding" immediately signaled a reply. But it was only the server returning his message as "undeliverable" since George had put no address on the e-mail. George reasoned, however, that if God were truly out there, He surely got the message.

Blind Chance: Just what in the Inconsequentiality do you think you're doing!

Random Number 1314: Well, like I told Mr. Chaos, once I got to know Purpose, there was no going back. I got tired of Pointlessness nagging at me all the time. I thought, "Who needs it?" And Misery—he may love company, but no one enjoys *his*. I guess what I'm saying is that this job was not all it was cracked up to be.

Blind Chance: Traitor! And to think your father was a Prime Number. I don't understand what has happened to you.

Random Number 1314: You can insult me all you want, but you won't change my mind.

Blind Chance: If you walk out now, don't bother ever coming back.

Random Number 1314: I have no desire to.

Blind Chance: You'll end up a fraction—or worse!

Random Number 1314: Have a nice day.

Blind Chance: My Entropy, how I hate that expression! How about you, Chaos? Chaos?

But Chaos made no reply as he longingly watched Random Number 1314's exit.

Sylvan Dream had really been Jeremiah's band. Ann had been the lead vocalist—the front person and a rising star in the local music scene. But while she may have had some minor drawing power, Jeremiah was the driving force. His spirit and creativity energized and transformed the band into something that caused people to talk.

Ann was not even sure why she got involved in the first place. Her background had been mostly in classical music and Broadway show tunes, not progressive rock. But perhaps the fact that it was so different was what appealed to her.

They met in college while Ann was working on her Master of Fine Arts degree. Jeremiah was only a sophomore academically (though it was his third year) and, while they had never been formally introduced, she had seen him around the conservatory.

Late one Friday afternoon, Ann saw Jeremiah carrying equipment into the small auditorium. It was right after midterm and most of the burned-out students had already left the building to start their weekend.

Ann smiled and said "Hi," but had fully intended to walk on by when he said, "I saw you in *Oklahoma* the other night. You were great." There was an intensity in the way he said that which she should have recognized but did not.

"Why thank you," she said, still intending to walk on by.

"I'm Jeremiah Callahan," he said. "But my friends call me Jerry or Jay or whatever."

"Nice to meet you Jeremiah Jerry Jay Whatever Callahan," said Ann. "I'm Ann—"

"I know who you are," he said. And this should have been Ann's second clue, but she missed it as well. "I'm starting a band. We're getting ready to practice. Would you like to come and hear us?"

"I really should be going . . ." she said.

"Just for a few minutes?" Jeremiah said with a fervency in his voice that was difficult to resist—not to mention that he was obviously a fan, which seemed in itself to create a sense of obligation. So she relented.

A few minutes turned into three hours before Ann realized it. Jeremiah introduced her to the other members of the band as they were setting up the equipment. They started playing and the next thing Ann knew she had a microphone in her hand and was singing with them. They played a variety of music—some current Top-40 songs, some old rock-and-roll standards, and even a couple of original songs that Jeremiah had written.

Ann was surprised at how much she enjoyed the evening. No audience. No pressure. Just music for the fun of it. She ignored her suspicion that she had been set up (a suspicion that turned out to be true). And she did not even mind that there was something mysterious—and maybe even a bit dangerous—about Jeremiah himself. It was an exciting diversion from the otherwise dull monotony of graduate school. Thus, Sylvan Dream was born.

A few weeks later, they set up their equipment on the concrete landing outside of the conservatory. Curious students stopped and listened. Some of the less inhibited danced in the parking lot, a good way to keep warm as the weather had turned chilly. When word about the band started getting around, they began playing at local nightclubs. It was a happy and relatively carefree time for Ann and part of her would have liked to see it go on and on. And, if not for two significant events that happened in the spring of the following year, her life might have turned out very differently.

The first was that Ann's father began feeling poorly that winter. Initially, he shrugged it off as whatever bug that was going around that he just could not shake. But when his symptoms worsened, he underwent a battery of tests. And then came the unexpected diagnosis—inoperable liver cancer.

The other significant event was near the opposite end of the emotional spectrum—not quite to the pole of ecstasy, but well within the range of happy and pleasant: she met George Weckbaugh.

As death is one of the inevitabilities of life, so, too, are statistics one of the inevitabilities of academic life. Ann was one of those people for whom it was difficult to say—between death and statistics—which was the worse fate.

It was not long after she learned of her father's illness that she was sitting in the corner of the computer lab, which was nearly vacant at that late hour. She was frustrated over the computer's apparent lack of cooperation and forlorn at being so far away from her family while her father was suffering.

George had been sent by Bailey Brothers, Inc., to upgrade the card reader when the pretty girl in the corner caught his fancy. A tear rolling down her cheek glistened in the harsh fluorescent light. And, like sad princesses in fairy tales, her sadness enhanced her beauty, while her beauty served to make her sadness all the more poignant. And as he watched her there, it was as if an arrow pierced his own heart.

George sauntered over, trying to look nonchalant. Ann took no notice of him until he said dryly, "I have a hammer in my toolbox, if you'd like to borrow it."

"Pardon me?" she said, mildly startled.

"I mean," said George, "it occurs to me that a couple of strategically placed blows would render this terminal inoperable."

The Life of Your Time

"Why on earth would I want to do that?" she said, trying, though not very successfully, to regain her composure.

"Just a guess," said George.

"So what if I did smash it?" said Ann.

"Maybe you'd feel better," said George.

"Then I'd get kicked out of school," said Ann.

"No you wouldn't," said George with a smile. "I'd fix it and then no one would ever know."

"Come to think of it, maybe getting kicked out of school's not such a bad idea, after all," said Ann, who soon found herself pouring out her heart to this total stranger.

George listened intently until she finished. "I'm no doctor," said George sympathetically. "But I do know a little about statistics."

"Oh, really?"

"I'm not in the habit of telling people what to do," said George. "But it looks to me that if you change that line of code right there, it might run better."

"How do you know?"

"I was monitoring it remotely from over there," he said pointing. "I saw when it blew up."

"I see," said Ann, not sure if she should be offended that he was "eavesdropping" on her program.

"But maybe you'd rather be left alone," said George. Sensing that he may have crossed some line he was not supposed to cross with her, he started to rise.

"Oh, no," she said, realizing how much she really did not want to be alone as well as how silly it was for her to be upset over his monitoring of her computer program (which apparently was his job and he was only trying to be helpful) when she had just voluntarily told him practically her whole life history. "Please stay."

Behind the Seen

Thus Ann formed two relationships that year with men who could not have been more different—one a younger man and the other considerably older. With Jeremiah, it was bright lights, youthful energy and high intensity. With George, it was mellow evenings and quiet, witty conversations. Despite their differences, Jeremiah and George shared at least one thing in common as far as Ann was concerned: she had no intention of becoming romantically involved with either one of them.

Then, without warning, a day of decision was thrust upon her. She was aware that Jeremiah was having stormy times at home—that his father wanted him to quit wasting so much time on music and concentrate on his business classes. But she did not know it had gone so far until one day he called to her across the grassy quadrangle near the center of campus, "Ann! Wait up!"

"What is it?" she asked. "What's wrong?"

"I'm leaving," he said breathlessly. "The old man and I had it out last night and it's come down to this: Either I leave now and follow my dream out on the road or I'm going to end up wearing a suit and tie every day and counting beans with my Dad for the rest of my life."

"You can't leave now," said Ann. "What about school?"

"Forget school," he said.

"What about the band?"

"I've already talked to the guys," Jeremiah said. "They're as excited as I am about going out on the road and making a name for ourselves. It's now or never."

"I see," she said, her voice flat. She wondered just how enthusiastic the band really was, but realized it

The Life of Your Time

was pointless trying to reason with a dreamer like Jeremiah. "So, then, this is goodbye?"

"Not if you come with us."

"Thanks for asking," she said, surprised at how cross her tone sounded. "Nice to know you included me somewhere in your plans. Where was I when you were making them?"

"You're always in my plans," he said with disarming earnestness.

"What do you mean by that?" she asked, softening a little.

"I mean that I love you," he said. "Since the moment I first saw you. Before we even met."

Ann was greatly taken aback at this revelation. She could not honestly say that she suspected nothing, as she had caught him staring at her more than once. But she had dismissed it as nothing more than a school-boy crush—a fleeting fancy that, like a soap bubble floating on the breeze, would soon pop and vanish.

This, however, sounded far more serious. She had not guessed that his feelings ran so deep. "I don't know what to say," she replied and truly she did not because everything between them had instantly changed.

"You don't have to say anything," said Jeremiah. "Just come with us—with me, I mean. I know this seems sudden. But sometimes life comes rushing at you and you have to grab it with both hands and hold on before it gets away from you."

Unexpectedly, Ann found herself on the verge of saying "yes." The road beckoned. Stardom called her name. She looked at him in the fading light in a way she had never looked at him before. In a matter of a moment, her passion for him that had, unknown to her, been smoldering for many months ignited.

Behind the Seen

Ann knew it made no sense that she should feel this way. She should have been insulted by such a clumsy, self-centered proposition. But that did not stop her feelings. Something about him was undeniably alluring.

Just as she was about to succumb, though, she thought of her father, suffering and struggling for his very life. She thought, too, of her new-found friend George who made her smile and coached her through statistics class. Saying "yes" to Jeremiah would mean saying goodbye to everything else she held dear. What she most wanted was to hold on to what she had and that, in the balance, outweighed the lure of adventure.

Ann put her hands on each of his cheeks and held his face tightly as she kissed him—slowly, passionately, and in plain view of everyone who happened to be watching. It was a kiss full of pent-up emotion over the things that had been and, moreover, the things that would never be.

Finally, she pulled away slightly, but still held her face close to his. Looking straight into his eyes, she said, "I'll never forget you, Jeremiah. I hope you find what you're searching for."

Then Ann turned and walked away, sobbing as she went. Jeremiah stood watching after her in stunned silence.

And that was the moment—the exact moment—upon which the rest of her life had turned. The look on Jeremiah's face and the infinite possibilities of what might have been had haunted her all those years. It was not that she had a bad life. It was that the good life she had in reality could not compete with the unlimited fantasy life of the path she chose not to take.

The Life of Your Time

Suddenly, and with clarity, she saw the unfairness and unfruitfulness of such a comparison. Regret was a wasting disease, she thought. It robs the spirit of joy like cancer robs the body of life. And she vowed right then and there she would have no more of it.

Ann drained the dishwater, dried her hands and hung her apron in the utility room. Then she went into the living room where George was sitting contemplatively in his favorite chair.

Sitting down on George's lap, Ann put her arms around his neck and whispered, "I am so glad that I have you for my husband." And then she kissed him.

George raised his eyebrows in wonder and thought, "God does move in mysterious ways!"

* * * * *

On a typical autumn Sunday afternoon, Terry McKinzie would be deeply engrossed in a football game. But that was not a typical Sunday afternoon for Terry.

After lunch, he led Kate into the living room and sat her down on the couch. He knelt down beside her on the floor and said, "Kate, there's something we need to talk about."

Instinctively, Kate feared the worst. *Here it comes,* she thought as her mind shifted into defense mode. *He wants a divorce. I just know it. That's why he's being so nice—so I won't take him to the cleaners in the settlement.*

"I've been doing a lot of thinking this weekend—about us," Terry continued. Kate covered her mouth with her hand lest her quivering lip betray her apprehension. "I'm not sure exactly how to say this, but you and I both know things haven't been what they ought

Behind the Seen

to be between us. And, well, I think it's time for a change. This isn't easy for me to say but . . ."

Dear God, no! thought Kate, fighting back the spasms that were swelling within her like a dam ready to burst. *Please don't let him say what I think he's going to say . . .*

"It's my fault," said Terry. "I've been a jerk. A real jerk. I admit it. And well, I'm sorry. Very sorry. Sorrier than you could possibly imagine. And I'm going to change. I'm going to be a better husband. You deserve better. And for starters, I got us tickets to the Monet grand opening next weekend. I'm going to rent a tux and the whole works. We'll have a great . . . "

At this point, Kate burst into tears, which was hardly the reaction Terry was expecting. "Uh-oh," he thought. "Now I've gone and made things worse instead of better."

But then she flung her arms around his neck, bumping his chin slightly in the process. He grimaced but suppressed the "Ouch!" He definitely did not want to spoil the moment.

Terry had finally come to the realization that he wasn't going to buy his way out of the doghouse with a trinket as he had tried to do so many times in the past. He knew his deplorable and nearly disastrous behavior as a husband needed more than a cosmetic fix. He needed to make some very fundamental changes in his life and he was determined to do so.

Kate cried for a good long time as they held each other tightly. The only sound in the room other than her gentle sobs was the tick, tick, ticking of the mantle clock, which seemed to linger for an inordinately long time at 1:14.

* * * * *

The Life of Your Time

The path between Percival's house and the Colonel's led past the school. The grade of the road at that point was actually about twenty feet above the schoolyard and separated from it by a steep, brushy embankment, providing a view that overlooked the athletic practice field.

Percival paused and stared down at a game of touch football in progress. He spotted Karen Maddox, playing quarterback on one of the teams. The center hiked the ball to her. She stepped back, faked a short pass and then threw a long, tight spiral for a touchdown.

"What an arm," thought Percival, as Karen's teammates congratulated her. And then, "What a girl."

The thought intimidated him—not that she was a girl, but that she seemed so confident and competent at whatever she did. Wherever she was, whatever she was involved in, Karen appeared to be perfectly at home.

This was not a feeling Percival shared. Looking down at the other children playing, he felt like they were part of a different world to which he really did not belong. It was like looking at one of those little glass-bubble snow scenes, so inviting yet so inaccessible. He tried to imagine what it would be like to enter the bubble and just play and be carefree and not to worry about things that happen to make a person wonder. But then he thought that if he once got in, someone or something outside the bubble might come along and give that world a good shake. Maybe it was that thought or maybe just the brisk breeze that made him shudder. He wished he knew what purpose, if any, might move the hand of the shaker.

As he contemplated this, the fresh breeze at his back seemed not so fresh, as if the bad intent of a universal conspiracy had become a palpable odor.

Behind the Seen

"What do you think you're doing?" said a voice that startled Percival so much that he almost fell off his bicycle. With a sinking feeling, he recognized the speaker was Freddie Lake and wheeled around to see Freddie and Billy Smith flanking him on their bikes. In response to the question, Percival shrugged his shoulders.

Freddie was the cherub-faced son of a prominent banker, with a mean streak that came and went depending on who was watching. He was also one of the bigger kids in the class, as Percival was now observing to his dismay.

That Freddie socialized with Billy might seem odd at first glance. After all, Freddie was one of the more popular students in Percival's class, while Billy came from, let us say, one of the less-well-groomed families of Central City. It might be helpful to note, though, that although Freddie was popular, he was not particularly well liked (popularity being a measure of how people act when you are around and being liked an indication of how they think about you when you are not around).

In Freddie's case, wealth and good looks did not quite overcome his personality which, tending to rely far too heavily on these attributes, was left severely deficient in some key qualities. In many respects Freddie was rather an opposite case from Percival. While the latter, being extraordinarily polite, was difficult to dislike but easy to ignore, the former, owing to the prominence of his position and deficiency in character, was easy to dislike but impossible to ignore.

Billy, then, was a companion of necessity for Freddie—someone who would do his dirty work for him, such being something for which he seemed well suited (beyond the literal meaning), being strong of body and weak of conscience. He came from a poor family and, while he did not particularly like Freddie either, (his mind not being well suited to such sentiments), he could at least appreciate the fact that Freddie was rather free with his money.

"I said, 'What are you doing?'" Freddie repeated.

"Just riding my bike," said Percival.

"Looks to me like you're spying," said Freddie.

"Yeah, spying," said Billy.

"And what do you think you were doing crowding in line on Friday?" said Freddie.

Billy echoed, "Yeah, what do you think you were doing?"

Freddie shot Billy an unmistakable look. Billy was good at beating people up, but of the fine art of interrogation, he was not a connoiseur.

"It was my turn to be line leader," offered Percival weakly.

"No one pushes ahead of me," Freddie said with an ever more threatening tone. Freddie and Billy inched their bikes menacingly closer.

Percival made no reply. He was trapped—the enemy in front and a steep, brushy drop-off behind.

"Looks like we're going to have to teach you a lesson in manners," said Freddie, bolstered by the fear he sensed in Percival.

Predator and prey. Survival of the fittest. Might makes right. Justice according to the laws of the jungle. But perhaps there could have been another law at work that day—one on which the irony of the most obnoxious kid in school purporting to teach a lesson in manners to the most extraordinarily polite was not lost. You might go so far as to say that it was a justice that appreciated a deeper sense of irony of its own.

Freddie nodded at Billy, who put his kickstand down and started to dismount. Percival wheeled his

Behind the Seen

bike around and steered it—of all places—off the embankment!

The ride was a rough one. Brambles grabbed at his jeans as he dodged rocks and small trees. Near the bottom he spotted a fallen tree just in time. At the last possible instant, he pulled back hard on the handlebars and managed to get the front wheel over it. The back wheel hit hard and he nearly lost control, but somehow he maintained his balance and safely reached the playground.

"After him!" cried Freddie, by which he meant that Billy should go first.

Billy did not seem to have full appreciation of the peril of this and bailed off behind Percival. But no sooner had he started down than his front tire hit some loose rocks and he laid the bike over on its side.

Freddie followed tentatively behind, though it was impossible to go slowly because of the steepness of the hill, so he picked up speed as he went. He might have made it if he had not glanced back to see if Billy was coming (Freddie being the kind of person who greatly preferred the odds of two-to-one over one-to-one). Thus, Freddie did not see the log. When his front wheel hit the bike stopped, but Freddie did not. He flipped over the handlebars, turned a three-quarters somersault in the air and landed flat on his back gasping for air.

Karen heard Freddie and Billy shouting and looked up to see them getting slowly to their feet and dusting themselves off. Then she saw Percival racing like the wind through the middle of their football game.

"Nice pass," he called to Karen when he whizzed by, as if everything in the picture was perfectly normal.

The Life of Your Time

"There is definitely something strange about that boy," she thought to herself as she watched him disappear around the school building.

* * * * *

Col. Martin's house turned out to be a neat little bungalow on Oak Street. A kindly-faced woman, whom Percival correctly assumed was Mrs. Colonel, opened the door. She welcomed him into their home and showed him into the den where, moments before, the Colonel had been reclining in his easy chair, reading the Sunday paper and drifting precariously close to the edge of a nap.

It had not occurred to Percival until that moment that by just dropping in uninvited, he might be imposing—maybe even impolite. After all, VIPs do not necessarily take kindly to boys they do not know well coming to their home uninvited at nap time. He suppressed a sudden urge to salute, though he did stand at rigid attention.

"Well, Percival," said the Colonel warmly. "What a pleasant surprise. Uh, at ease, soldier."

Col. Martin offered him the sofa across the low coffee table from the recliner, while Mrs. Colonel excused herself to make hot chocolate. A long bookshelf took up most of the far wall, while the adjacent wall was covered with photos of airplanes and military memorabilia. Had his mind not been so preoccupied, Percival would have been glad to spend hours just browsing through it all. But today he had a purpose. The Colonel could sense his intensity so he said, in a voice with more than a hint of southern drawl, "What's on your mind, son?"

"Well, sir," Percival began. "I was wondering if you could tell me about God."

Behind the Seen

"That's a pretty big subject," said Col. Martin, appreciating afresh the wonderful directness of children. He was of the opinion that there was far too much "beating around the bush" in the world. "Is there something specific you would like to know?"

"So, you do believe there is a God?" asked Percival, thinking it was best to establish first things first.

"Yes. Do you?"

"I believe in something," said Percival. "But what I would like to know is what kind of God is He? Like the story you told this morning about Daniel and the lions. Does He still do stuff like that?"

"The only lions I've ever seen were in a zoo, so I can't speak from direct experience about that," the Colonel said with a smile. Then he grew more serious and leaned forward in his chair. "But if you want to know if He is the kind of God you can depend on when people are shooting at you or when your plane's on fire and you're losing altitude fast and you know you're going to crash, then the answer is definitely yes."

"Did you see Him?" asked Percival.

"Who? God? No."

"Then how did you know it was Him?"

"It's hard to explain, Percival. I just knew."

"Hmmm," said Percival. "The reason I want to know is that something strange happened to me—and my Dad, too. I've been trying to figure out if it means anything."

"Tell me about it."

So Percival related the events of the past few days. He went into great detail because he was afraid that if he left out something it might muddle the interpretation. Col. Martin listened attentively and, by the time Percival was finished, so was the hot chocolate which Mrs. Martin served. Then she left again so they could talk man to man.

The Life of Your Time

The Colonel pondered Percival's tale for a long moment, trying to figure out where to begin and how to explain it in terms Percival could understand. Finally, an idea came to him. "So you are a writer."

"Just barely, sir," said Percival.

"But you have a notion of what being a writer is about."

"Yes, I think so."

"Well, let's talk about God in those terms," said the Colonel. "Consider that God is an Author and the whole universe is a story that He has written and all the people in the world are the characters of His story. Can you imagine that?"

Percival nodded and Col. Martin continued. "Now as the Author of this big story, God has complete freedom to write it however He wants to—all the people, all the scenes, all the events are completely under His control. There is nothing that is just a coincidence or an accident. So, in that sense, the things that happened to you and your Dad do mean something because they happened in God's story."

Percival felt vindicated. Perhaps he had not just been making something out of nothing after all.

"Now real life is different than a book," the Colonel said. "In a book the characters think and say and do precisely what the author tells them. But real people have free will. They make their own decisions about what they're going to do. You might say that real life is more like a play—more complicated because the actors can choose whether they want to follow the Author's script."

"All the world's a stage," said Percival. "My Mom told me somebody famous said that."

"That's it, yes," said the Colonel. "So just imagine a gigantic theater where God is going to stage an epic play—The History of the World—and He's looking for

Behind the Seen

actors and actresses to cast into the roles. There are plenty of parts to go around and every one of them is very important and every single person can have a part. But there's one requirement that everyone in the cast must meet. It's not that they must have acting experience or even any acting talent at all. No, for His cast, God is looking for people who are sincerely devoted to Him as Author and Director. Although He already knows who they are because He knows everything, He thinks it best to let them discover it for themselves. So He devises a test of sorts."

"A test?" said Percival, not sure if he liked the sound of that.

"Not like a test at school," said Colonel Martin. "This is a test of people's hearts. God sets the stage which is the world and leaves behind the script—which is his Word—while He Himself watches unseen from the balcony. Now this is a very unique Script, unlike any other, because it's not so much about telling the cast what to say and do, but more about what the Author is like and what kind of people He is looking for."

"Do they pass the test?" asked Percival.

"Some do," said the Colonel. "But some ignore the Script and just do their own thing—whatever pleases them. Others scoff at the idea that there is any Author at all—that the stage is just an illusion and the Script is a hoax. Since the Author is unseen, there is never a shortage of people who want to take charge and push themselves forward to the front of the stage. Just like at school, there are always kids who want to crowd ahead of you in line."

"I know what you mean."

"But then, the most amazing thing of all happens," said Colonel Martin. "The Author writes Himself into the play! Tragically, the people reject Him and put

Him to death. A few, however, recognize Him for Who He is and follow Him wholeheartedly. From that time on, there is a sharp division among the players about the identity of the Author. The Author, who has returned to the balcony, takes careful note of the players who are devoted to Him. His followers wait expectantly because the Script says the Author is going to return very soon and all who love the Author will be with Him forever. Does that make any sense to you?"

"Sort of," Percival said. "But where do I fit into all this?"

"Everything in this world—the way it is made and the way things happen, is designed to point people to the Author. Unfortunately, most people are so wrapped up in themselves that they miss what He is saying to them. But you've been given a tremendous gift, Percival, because God has opened your eyes to see that there is a lot more going on around us than most people ever realize. It's hard to tell if the specific incident has any special significance because He reaches different people in different ways. Occasionally, He uses something really spectacular—a blinding light or a burning bush or the many miraculous healings that Jesus performed. But for most of us, it's more subtle— a powerful sermon, a special song, an act of kindness, or a cry for help in a time of distress. The issue is not *how* God gets your attention but that He *does* and you respond to it. Although, now that I think about it . . . ." His voice trailed off.

"What is it, sir?" said Percival anxiously.

"1314 is military time for 1:14," said Col. Martin. "It does make you wonder, doesn't it."

"Wow!" said Percival. "But what does it mean?"

"I honestly don't know," said the Colonel. "But when I think of 1:14, what comes to my mind is a

Behind the Seen

Bible verse—John 1:14: 'The Word became flesh and made his dwelling among us.' It means that the God who created the whole universe became a man—Jesus—so that we could know Him and have a relationship with Him. And just like He has given meaning and purpose to the universe, He gives meaning and purpose and eternal life to all who believe in Him and follow Him."

Percival sat in silence for a long moment and then said slowly, "So the meaning of life is not an answer—it's a person."

"You could put it that way," the Colonel said thoughtfully. "In fact, I don't think I've ever heard it stated better."

There was another long pause while Percival let all this sink in. Col. Martin resisted the temptation to say more or press for a response. Although he was not a particularly patient man by nature, he knew in his heart that he had done all he could do for the moment. It was out of his hands now.

Percival slowly rose to his feet. "I probably should be getting home now, before my parents start worrying."

As he walked Percival to the door, Col. Martin wondered what would become of him. On the edge of life, on the edge of eternity, his soul hung in the balance. How many came to that point, but stopped short of taking that all-important next step? He could only wonder and pray that would not be Percival's fate.

A thousand thoughts intruded on Percival's mind between the den and the front door, all demanding attention at once. He thought of the strange incident with the clock. Was it just a—what did Mrs. Thomas call it? Oh, yes, a coincidence. He definitely needed to look that word up when he got home.

The Life of Your Time

And cutting in line, thought Percival. Miss Pickett would have been so disappointed if she would have known the truth. Come to think of it, he was disappointed in himself for having done it. What would Mr. Wimbley say about that, he thought. Maybe he did have a head injury. Or seizures. His mind certainly seemed jumbled up these days. And what was the matter with the Clock Man this morning? He looked like he had just seen Bigfoot. And Mom—why was she so sad all the time? And why did that number keep popping up everywhere? And what was the deal with Dad's computer? And what did any of this have to do with the meaning of life? For that matter, did life have to have any meaning at all?

It was a deep thought. A profound thought. A thought far beyond his ability to comprehend.

But somehow, as soon as he thought this thought, he knew the answer had to be "yes." It was as if in a special place in his heart, a light was kindled. Suddenly, things started to make a great deal of sense.

As he reached the door, Percival turned to the Colonel and said simply, "I believe."

Epilogue

After Taste

Narrator: I like that part.
Author: Thank you.
Narrator: Are we ready for the conclusion?
Author: I think so, yes.
Narrator: Percival went straight home and told his parents. He introduced them to Col. Martin and his wife (Thelma was her name) and they all became fast friends. As far as he knew, George's computer never did anything else it was not programmed to do. But he did not worry about that, however, because he found a link to God that was more direct than computer circuits. He quickly became consumed by a passion for studying the Script and even taught himself ancient Greek. Ann, who had rediscovered the most important reason of all to sing, joined the choir at church and performed solos often, much to the people's delight.
Doug Martin continued his successful career in college football and even made it to the professional level. More importantly, he went on to a highly successful marriage with Nancy Chandler.

The Life of Your Time

Terry McKinzie upheld his pledge to be a better husband to Kate. Accordingly, he lost no time finding Marla Roberts a job at a bigger market station in the city, which is all she ultimately wanted anyway. He also bought a battery for his watch and used it regularly to remind himself to leave work at a decent hour each day.

Rick Callaway struggled to fight his dragon in many ways. But the fact that he was struggling at all instead of giving up was in itself a vast improvement. A short time later, he set out in search of his brother Jeremiah, though the odds against finding him were not in his favor. Jeremiah's way was a downward winding path that was many years cold. Nevertheless, against the advice of his friend Doug, who did not think he was ready, Rick undertook the difficult journey.

Professor Funkmeyer agreed to keep his metaphysical opinions to himself and returned to the university. He did, however, spend the majority of his free time trying to develop a mathematical model for self-organizing systems, though as far as anyone knows, he never came up with anything conclusive.

Mr. Wimbley, the school counselor, never really accomplished much of anything. But the important thing was that he felt very good about his career.

Random Number 1314 went to work for Significance and found his new occupation very satisfying. Soon after 1314 left the disorganization, Chaos reportedly fell to pieces and was said to be seriously considering a career move himself.

As for Percival, he fulfilled his promise to Karen Maddox by telling her that he did have the meaning-of-life thing figured out: It was not an answer,

After Taste

it was person. Although she was skeptical at first, she eventually became a believer, too. And their relationship—well that, as you may suspect, is a story in itself. Suffice to say that Percival did pursue a career in writing, not just for the *Central Citizen* newspaper, but for the Central Citizen of the Universe!

* * * * *

Author: Well told!
Narrator: So, you did not mind my occasional embellishments?
Author: Oh, no. Well, except maybe for the parts where you made me sound better than I really am. I probably should go back and edit some of that out.
Narrator: You are too humble, sir.
Author: It's just that I don't want it to sound pretentious.
Narrator: It does not sound pretentious to me. But, then again, I have been accused of being verbose and heavy-handed.
Author: I prefer to think of you as a highly articulate person with strong convictions.
Narrator: Why thank you! It has been a pleasure working with you, Mr. Weckbaugh.
Author: Please, call me Percival.

Coming soon from this author . . .

The Chronicles Of Japheth
By Steven J. Byers

An eyewitness account of the events leading up to the greatest catastrophe in human history as seen through the eyes of Noah's son Japheth.